HOME on the RANCH

HOME *on the* RANCH

HOW TO LASSO A COWBOY

— ✠ —

CHRISTINE WENGER

HARLEQUIN® HOME ON THE RANCH

Recycling programs
for this product may
not exist in your area.

ISBN-13: 978-1-335-45339-6

How to Lasso a Cowboy

Printed in U.S.A.

Christine Wenger has worked in the criminal justice field for more years than she cares to remember, but now spends her time reading, writing and seeing the sights in our beautiful world. A native central New Yorker, she loves watching professional bull riding and rodeo with her favorite cowboy, her husband, Jim. You can reach Christine at PO Box 1823, Cicero, NY 13039, or through her website at christinewenger.com.

To my St. Margaret's, Ludden
and Powelson buddies, Janice Egloff DiFant
and Patty Tomeny Holgado.

Time sure flies, but we're still having fun!

Prologue

Jenna Reed studied the new clothes that she'd bought for her long-awaited trip to Europe. They were organized by day, stacked in neat piles on the bed in her guest room and her matched set of tomato-red luggage was open and ready to be filled.

She reread the now dog-eared itinerary that she'd received from Happy Singles Travel, Inc. She knew it by heart, but she still loved looking at it. Their motto was printed in lime green on the top of their letterhead: "Travel with us, meet new friends and discover new places."

She would have rather traveled with her

current friends, but they were all too tied up with their husbands and/or kids. Though she was disappointed, she understood. So, she was going with seventy-five other singles, mostly women, for three glorious weeks in Europe!

Finally, Jenna was going to live it up. She hadn't had a vacation since she'd started teaching fourth grade after college. When other teachers at Wilson Road Grammar School took the summer off, she worked summer school and tutored kids whenever she was asked. Among her peers, she was the teacher who never said no.

She loved teaching mostly because of the kids. She thought of them as *hers* and threw her whole being into her work. But they *weren't* her kids, and at age twenty-nine, she'd given up looking for Mr. Right. She just wanted Mr. Right *Now*. Someone special. Someone she could hang out with and who liked to do the same things that she did.

She'd once wanted to settle down and have children, but all that changed when she approached her thirtieth birthday. With no romantic prospects, she decided that she had too much living to do—and *now* was the time for her to enjoy life. So she cut her workload and began making plans to change her life from a humdrum, staid existence to one of excitement and adventure.

As part of her new life plan, Jenna decided to make a drastic career change and applied for a year-long position teaching English in China. Every time she thought of her application being accepted and making a move, excitement shot through her.

Even if she didn't get the position, she'd take a leave of absence and travel, visiting places that she'd only read about. And this European vacation would be the perfect start to her new plan.

Jenna sat on the edge of the bed, holding on to her itinerary, and imagined meeting her knight in shining armor at a bistro in Paris or at the Parthenon in Greece. Maybe he'd strike up a conversation with her as she watched him maneuver his yacht through the glittering waters of Cannes or bump into him on the Rialto Bridge in Venice.

Wherever her mystery man was, she wanted him to know that she'd be landing at Heathrow Airport in London in exactly seven days, ten hours and thirty-two minutes.

The phone rang, startling her our of her daydream. She rushed to pick it up.

"Hey, sis."

"Tom! How are you?"

Calling her brother was on her list of things to do. She'd planned on letting him know when she was leaving on her trip. Then her excitement dissolved. Her brother only called her when he needed something or if it was bad news. She braced herself.

"I called about Andy—" he began.

She just adored her ten-year-old nephew. "Oh, Tom! Is he okay?"

"Relax, Jenna. He's fine. He just didn't do well on his final report card. He's failing reading and math. He's going to be held back in fourth grade unless he goes to summer school."

"That's too bad."

"Yup." There was a moment of silence. "And since he could use some extra help, I thought of you, since you teach fourth grade. I figure if you came down here to Tucson, you could tutor him and babysit at the same time. I've been helping him myself, but I'm not doing that great of a job. He's not getting it."

"I'm sure he's getting it, Tom. You're a very patient father."

Then something hit her—Tom had said *babysit*.

"Uh… Tom, why do you need me to baby-sit? Where are you going to be?"

"As long as you're going to be here at the Bar R, I figured that I could enter as many bronc-and bull-riding events as I can during the summer. It'd be the perfect opportunity for me to win some extra money, pay for some repairs that I need to do around my ranch. Besides, Andy needs braces, his baby-sitters are costing me a fortune and Marla just filed for divorce. I need to retain a lawyer."

Jenna was silent. She knew that Tom was still reeling from his wife leaving him for another man. Marla said that traveling the bull-riding circuits kept him away from home too much.

"When do you need me?" Jenna asked.

"Next week."

"Tom—" Jenna's heart sank. Her brother never asked for anything, and she owed him so much. "I meant to call you, but time just got away from me. I'm supposed to leave for Europe on vacation this Tuesday. I'll be gone for three weeks, but—"

There were no buts. She'd do anything for Tom and Andy. After their mother and father

died in a terrible auto accident when Tom
was a senior and she was a freshman in high
school, Tom assumed the role of parent even
though they lived with their grandparents.
It was Tom, the champion bull rider, who'd
helped her with her college tuition. It was
Tom who loaned her the money for a down
payment on her house when she got her teaching job in Phoenix.

And Andy was the sweetest nephew an
aunt could have, and Jenna knew that Tom
needed the extra money. Besides, she didn't
want Andy to have trouble in school.

She sighed. Her European vacation was
spinning down the toilet, but her family
needed her. Still, she held on tighter to her
itinerary, not wanting to part with it.

"Sis, I understand. I can make other arrangements."

"Don't you dare," Jenna said adamantly. "I
can postpone my trip." She'd waited this long
to spread her wings, she could wait a little
longer. "And I took out travel insurance, so
there's really no problem."

She stared at the new clothes that she'd
bought throughout the year, just for this trip.
The clothes were totally inappropriate for the
summer at Tom's ranch in Tucson. She'd need

old shirts, old shorts and even older jeans. And her beat-up old cowboy boots. If Tom wasn't going to be around, she'd probably have to do some work around his ranch, too. And she sure as hell didn't need her new navy raincoat in the Arizona desert.

"A week from today, then," Jenna said. "I'll drive down in the morning, and get there around noon. Is that okay?" Instead of flying to Europe on that day, she'd be driving to Tom's ranch.

She could hear Tom let out a relieved breath. "I can't thank you enough. I really appreciate this."

"It'll be great to spend time with Andy," she said, meaning every word. "How long are you going to be gone, Tom?"

"As long as I can. And as long as Andy is okay with me being gone. He'll be thrilled that you're going to come for a visit, so he won't miss me all that much. I had a little talk with him and prepared him in case you said yes, and he understood. He said that he was going to root for me and Uncle Dustin on television."

"Uncle" Dustin Morgan wasn't Andy's real uncle. He was an old friend of Tom's from high school. The two had been traveling together from rodeo to rodeo for years.

Every time she talked with Andy, most of the conversation centered on Dustin, a man she'd thought about with steady frequency since she'd first laid eyes on him in algebra class in freshman year at Catalina High School in Tucson.

"Uh…um…" Tom began. "Speaking of Dustin, I invited him to come and stay at the ranch when he's released from the hospital. He needs to heal up a bit from his accident."

Jenna knew from watching the Albuquerque event on TV that Dustin seriously injured his ankle when a bull stepped on him. She worried about his injury and worried even more when the sports medicine doctor for the bull riders stated that he was being taken to a nearby hospital for emergency surgery.

But wait…was Tom expecting her to take care of Dustin? He couldn't possibly think that she'd know what to do. She was a teacher, not a nurse.

"Tom, you asked Dustin to stay at the ranch?" Her heart began racing when she realized that Dustin Morgan would be living under the same roof with her.

"Yeah. He's going to stay here with you

and Andy and look after the ranch for me. He won't be any trouble for you."

What she remembered about Dustin from high school was her intense crush on him, but she'd been too much of a geek to even relax around him. She'd longed to date him, but he was way too popular, and she was way too much of a bookworm for them to have anything in common.

The only thing they had in common was Tom, and Jenna couldn't wait until Tom brought Dustin over to their house.

Then she remembered the sadness she felt when he was offered a full ride—a complete, four-year scholarship to the University of Nevada at Las Vegas. Instead of accepting it, he'd hit the circuit to compete with the Professional Bull Riders. He never graduated with their senior class.

What a waste, she thought, although he made a small fortune riding bulls.

"Dustin can help you out with Andy, too," Tom added.

She was about to tell him that she didn't need any help with Andy, and that she'd feel uncomfortable practically living with Dustin Morgan, but it sounded like a done deal.

No trouble?

She doubted that.

"Thanks again, Jenna. You know I appreciate this, and so does Dustin. Andy will, too, when he passes to fifth grade."

"No problem, Tom," she lied. "See you next Monday."

They hung up, and Jenna just sat, reeling.

Looking down, she saw that she was still clutching her itinerary. Soon, she'd have to call and cancel her wonderful trip.

After a while, she lovingly placed the item into her brand-new tomato-red, twenty-nine-inch upright with the 360-degree wheels.

Maybe she had to cancel for now, but as soon as possible, she'd reschedule—just as soon as Tom figured out when he'd return. She was needed by her family, and that was okay.

But it seemed as though she was always needed, mostly by those she called the "four Ps": her pupils, their parents, the principal or her peers, and she always had to postpone her dreams of romance and adventure.

She sighed. Now, Dustin Morgan, fresh from the hospital, needed her.

Then she smiled as she began to pick up her clothes. She might still be a geek, and Dustin might be one of the most popular bull riders in the PBR, but maybe her stay at the Bar R would somehow give her a chance to spread her wings, just like she'd planned to do on her European trip.

And maybe…just maybe… Dustin would turn out to be the adventure of a lifetime.

Chapter One

Dustin Morgan struggled to get out of a taxi in front of Tom Reed's ranch house.

He tugged his crutches out of the vehicle and positioned them under his arms while the driver unloaded his duffel bag.

Unfortunately, in the short-go round in Albuquerque, a bucking, whirling, two-thousand-pound Brahma named Cowabunga bucked him off, then stomped on his ankle, crushing it. After surgery, Dustin sported a massive amount of hardware to keep his bones together, along with a heavy cast.

Damn it.

Thanks to Cowabunga, he'd have to skip the usually profitable summer circuit.

After a couple of years of always being a bridesmaid, he'd finally hit number one in the rankings, and now he couldn't ride. While he sat at home and watched the Professional Bull Riders on TV with his leg up, there'd be several young guns who would jump over him in the standings. But maybe, if everything went as planned, when he got back he could move up again in time for the PBR World Finals in Las Vegas in early November. Fingers crossed.

He paid the taxi driver, turned toward the house and took a hearty breath. He could smell the scent of animals on the air. Damn, how he loved that smell!

He was itching to do something where he could work up a sweat, but his surgeon had told him to take it easy. Dustin couldn't grasp that concept. There had never been a time when he'd taken it easy.

When he was younger, he entered junior rodeos and rode anything with fur. As a sophomore in high school, he played football and caught rodeos every chance he could. When he turned eighteen, he was able to qualify for the Professional Bull Riders circuit as well as the Professional Rodeo Cowboys Association. He rode bulls in the PBR. In the PRCA, he rode broncs.

And he'd managed to avoid serious injury—until now.

Dustin studied the long ranch house and the outbuildings of the Bar R Ranch. Someday, he'd have a spread like this.

He looked at his duffel bag lying on the Arizona dust. Dustin couldn't believe that he'd agreed to stay at Tom's place. The only thing that had convinced him to come here was the fact that Tom needed him—and to be honest, he owed Tom big time. Tom had saved his life two years ago by pushing him away from a rogue bull. His friend would always sport scars from being gored.

"I have a favor to ask of you," Tom had said when he'd visited Dustin in the hospital after his surgery.

Dustin had struggled to stay focused, still a little groggy from the painkillers he'd been given. "Hit me with it."

"Since you're going to be laid up for a while, how about heading to my ranch and overseeing the operation? I don't want you to work, just supervise the foreman and the hands. You're going to be recuperating any-way—how about doing it at the Bar R?"

"I—I don't—"

"My sister will be there taking care of Andy for me. And Andy would just love a visit from you. It's been a long time, Dustin."

"Jenna?" His eyelids drifted closed for a moment, but Jenna's image appeared in his mind. In high school lugging a load of books. Studying under the big tree by the school cafeteria while everyone else was having fun. Being elected class president every year for four years. Giving the valedictorian speech at graduation.

He'd always liked her energy, her sense of independence, her willingness to get involved and the fact that she was comfortable being alone and didn't follow the crowd, like he always had.

Back then, she'd had long blond hair that she usually wore in a ponytail tied with a piece of rawhide and usually pierced by at least one pen and one pencil. That was Jenna, always studying, always writing in a notebook. Her spring-green eyes were magnified by wire-rimmed glasses that rode low on her nose.

He'd spent many a high school class secretly watching her.

He'd wanted to talk to Jenna on numerous occasions—to ask her out—but he'd always thought that she wouldn't give him the time of day. It wasn't as if she was a snob—she was very friendly to everyone but him—so he figured that Tom had told her to stay away from him. Tom was very protective of Jenna after the death of his parents, and Dustin had to admit that he'd had many girlfriends. Jenna could see that for herself. But they were just friends—or they were buckle bunnies—and they weren't Jenna.

So, to get his Jenna fix, Dustin often went to Tom's house, not only to hang out with Tom, but to catch a glimpse of her, too.

"You're going to need someone to help you manage," Tom continued. "With your folks being in Alaska and your apartment on the third floor of a building without elevators, you don't have much of a choice. You help me, and Jenna will help you."

There was something wrong with his reasoning, but Dustin couldn't put his finger on it back at the hospital. If only Tom would leave so he could sleep.

Sleep…blessed sleep. The pain was exhausting him, and he didn't want to take too many pain pills if he could help himself.

"It's okay with Jenna," Tom said. "She's looking forward to seeing you again."

That struck Dustin as strange. He doubted if Jenna even remembered him from high school. He hadn't had a decent conversation with her in years. Matter of fact, the last time he'd talked to Jenna for any length of time was at Andy's christening ten years ago. He was Andy's godfather; Jenna was Andy's godmother.

Now, as he stood at the gate of Tom's ranch, he remembered the promise he'd made to Tom years ago—a promise he regretted to this day. He'd given his word to Tom that he'd stay away from Jenna. Therefore, his interaction with her was limited to fleeting glances and some short blips of conversation whenever she attended the PBR events.

He might as well be back in high school.

Dustin flung his duffel over his right shoulder and thought of Tom. When you traveled with a man to and from rodeos you got to know him really well. Tom was more than a good friend, he was like a brother, and he didn't want to betray Tom's trust.

Dustin had almost told Tom that he wasn't going to stay at his ranch to recuperate. He didn't want to be a burden on Jenna or on anyone. He could take care of himself—some-how, someway—but he hadn't been able to find his voice.

He remembered falling asleep, dreaming of spending the summer with pretty, smart Jenna Reed. In his dream, Jenna didn't think of him as the class clown, the class jock or as someone who didn't take advantage of a four-year scholarship to hit the road to ride bulls. She thought of him only as a man.

But this wasn't a dream. This was reality, and he was about to spend most of the summer with Jenna.

Then again, maybe it *was* a dream.

"Aunt Jenna?" Andy said sweetly. "Can I go outside now? I want to watch the guys break Maximus."

Jenna smiled and ran her fingers through her nephew's sandy hair. His blue eyes were wide with hope. How could math and reading compete with a bucking bronc?

"Do the first seven decimal problems and you can go. We'll do reading comprehension later."

She leaned over to Andy and pointed to the problems on page fifteen of his math book. She'd seen progress with Andy during the week that she'd been tutoring him, and she didn't want to lose the momentum.

She did the breakfast dishes as Andy labored over his workbook.

The doorbell rang. "I'll get it," Jenna said, walking into the living room to get the front door.

She looked through the peephole. Standing on the porch, propped up by a pair of crutches, was none other than Dustin Morgan.

His hair was darker than ever, and his eyes were as blue as the Arizona sky above. If possible, he looked better than he had in high school. Her cheeks heated just looking at him. TV didn't do him justice.

Jenna could never forget the guy who'd flirted with every girl in high school. That is, everyone but her.

He'd been a star quarterback and the best player on the basketball team in freshman and sophomore years as well as a rodeo champ. He had all the girls drooling over him, including her.

But he never paid her any attention. In fact, she was the only female he seemed to avoid.

And he'd turned down a full scholarship so

he could ride with the PBR. Jenna had never been able to understand this.

She swung the door open, and he smiled widely. Her gaze drifted to his crutches, his torn sweatpants and the cast that went from his foot to his knee.

"Hello, Dustin. It's been a while." She offered her hand. So far, so good.

He took her hand for several heartbeats and held it before he finally shook it. She could feel the calluses on his palms and fingers.

It was a simple thing, just a handshake, but at his touch, she felt like a giddy schoolgirl again instead of a levelheaded almost-thirty-year-old.

"It's good to see you again, Jenna."

He smiled warmly, and she could understand why a gaggle of buckle bunnies always vied for his attention.

"You, too. Although I see you on TV all the time at the bull riding events or…or…" She lost her train of thought for a moment. "But this arrangement is going to be…different."

Jenna could hear the quiver in her voice, and wondered why seeing Dustin up close and personal was unnerving her.

"I guess you're stuck with me," he said.

She pulled her hand away from his. Maybe

then she'd relax. "I—I guess I am," she blurted anxiously. Then, realizing what she said, she tempered her statement. "But you need help, and Tom said that you're going to oversee the ranch, so that'll help out. Besides, Andy is over-the-top thrilled that you're going to be here."

"It'll be fun to spend time with the little cowboy," he said.

She avoided his eyes and stared down at his cast and crutches. "I am sorry that you hurt your ankle. Cowabunga walked all over you."

He pushed back his cowboy hat with his thumb. "Thanks. It wasn't my best dismount, but I got lucky. It could have been a lot worse."

Jenna shuddered. "You did get lucky."

He shrugged. "You know what they say about bull riding—it's not *when* you'll get hurt, but how bad and how often."

An awkward pause hung in the air between them. Were they doomed to make innocuous small talk the entire summer?

"Let's go inside so you can sit down," she said. "I'll get your duffel."

"I can get it," he said quickly, scooping it up from the ground and then trying to get his crutches over the threshold.

She moved closer. "What can I do to help you?"

"Nothing. I can do it myself." She heard the edge in his voice.

What was she supposed to do to assist him? He seemed put out that she even offered to help.

They'd better figure out a way to exist in harmony. Didn't he understand that, for the most part, they'd be living together? She'd have to watch out for him, cook for him, do his laundry and help him get around on those crutches.

Would she have to help him bathe, too?

Her face heated in embarrassment and her heart raced at the thought of seeing Dustin Morgan naked.

Well, she'd wanted adventure and excitement, didn't she?

The cast was so awkward! It felt like he was lugging around an extra thirty pounds of dead weight. To make things worse, his duffel slipped off his shoulder, slid down his arm and crutch, and hit the floor of the porch.

He struggled to pick up the damn thing.

Jenna offered to help, but there was no way he wanted to impose on her—a woman that he barely knew but had adored from afar since high school. No way.

And there was that damn promise he'd made to Tom niggling at the back of his mind. Was this Tom's idea of a joke, having Jenna and him live together for several weeks? Or didn't Tom remember their conversation in the ambulance when Tom had saved Dustin's life?

Dustin remembered it very clearly.

"Thanks for saving my life, partner. I didn't see that bull heading for me. I owe you big-time," Dustin said.

"Forget it. You'd do the same to me. And the only thing you owe me is your promise."

Dustin held his breath. He knew what was coming.

"My sister. I see you looking at her." Tom winced in pain. "She's...not as...experienced as you are. She's been protected her whole life, first by my parents, then by me. You're like a brother, but you love the women too much. You'll hurt her, you know. And you know, you'll never be around for her, riding the circuit. She deserves someone who'll be home all the time."

Dustin looked at Jenna waiting for him to enter the house. He'd rather cut off his riding arm than hurt her, but his friend was right about him never being there for her—not when he was still riding—and he figured he had several good years left in him yet.

So Dustin renewed his promise to stay away from Jenna. But, again, maybe Tom had forgotten about it, or why else would he have asked him to stay at the ranch knowing that Jenna would be there?

As if on cue, Jenna snatched the duffel from him, and held the door open, giving him a wide berth to maneuver inside the living room.

Damn. He hated feeling like an invalid.

He should have holed up in his apartment, done things for himself. But the surgeon who'd operated told him that if he took it easy, he'd heal quicker, and he'd return to the PBR quicker.

That was his goal. He was poised to win the PBR World Finals in Vegas, and that was just what he was going to do. With the money he'd win, he could hang up his spurs and finally settle down on a ranch of his own.

That's what he'd been saving for all these years on the road. His own spread.

But first, he had to heal, and Tom had convinced him that this was the best place for him. Maybe it was—but being with Jenna 24/7 was a bonus.

"Uncle Dustin! Uncle Dustin!"

Andy came running into the living room of the Santa Fe-style house and stopped two feet from where Dustin had collapsed into a side chair and stretched out his leg.

"Hey, partner! How've you been?" He held out his hand, and Andy shook it. "It's been a long time."

"I see you on TV all the time, you and my dad. Oh, and J.R., and Skeeter, and Cody and Robson and Adriano and—"

Dustin laughed as Andy named the entire roster of riders. The boy couldn't be cuter. His eyes were bright blue, his hair sandy and he was probably taller than other kids his age. But ever since his mother had left, the spark had faded a bit from the boy's eyes.

"I think you've gotten taller," Dustin said.

Andy grinned. "Really?"

"I wouldn't say it if I didn't mean it."

As Andy read what his father and some of the other riders had written on Dustin's cast, the cowboy eyed Jenna, who was sitting on the couch opposite him.

She was more beautiful than he remembered, all wholesome and not made up like the buckle bunnies he often met on the circuit. Her blond hair tickled her chin, and turquoise stones dangled from her ears.

He glanced at his duffel. It barely had enough clothes for two days. He'd only packed it for the Albuquerque bull riding, not for a stay in the hospital or for a long stay at Tom's ranch. Beside it lay his crutches.

"I need to go shopping. All my clothes are in my apartment in Tubac," he said mostly to himself.

"You live in Tubac? The artist colony?" Jenna asked wide-eyed.

"Yep. That Tubac." He lived two floors above a shop that sold various types of jewelry, pottery and paintings.

"I'd be glad to drive you to your apartment," Jenna said.

"I don't want to impose on you any more."

Tubac was an hour's drive from Tucson. Maybe he could pay one of the ranch hands to drive him there and get some of his stuff.

He didn't tell Jenna that he painted western scenes—riders on bucking bulls and broncs. Cowboys mending fence. The saguaros and mountains around Tubac and Tucson. It had been just for fun at first, but then he'd started selling his work through some of the local craft shops.

"Well, I'd better show you the guest room," Jenna said, moving to hand him his crutches.

"I can do it."

Her perfume drifted around him—something light and flowery. It suited her.

"You're probably hungry, too. How about if I make you a sandwich or something?" Jenna asked.

"I promised Tom that I'd ramrod his ranch while I'm laid up. I'll try and stay out of your way and not bother you."

She shook her head. "It's not a bother, Dustin. I'm happy to help."

He was sure that she was trying to be polite, but he didn't intend to be a burden on her, or anyone. That wasn't his style. He was just here to help Tom while he was on the road, and he could do that on crutches.

And he was going to enjoy Jenna's company while he was here.

In spite of his injury, one good thing could come of it—he would finally get to know her better. But no matter how much he was still attracted to her, nothing would come of their close proximity—he'd see to that. He'd made a promise to Tom. And Dustin Morgan was a man of his word.

Jenna's senses were reeling as if she were back in high school. She tried to play it cool, just as she had back then, but her cool probably seemed standoffish.

Later, as she made Andy and Dustin ham-and-cheese sandwiches, she thought of Dustin's blue eyes—his sexy gaze was more intense than ever. His lips seemed more sensuous and his black hair looked even softer.

But his smile and good nature were what always charmed the high school girls. When he turned on his smile, flashing those whiter-than-white teeth, no female was immune.

Jenna had attended several PBR events through the years, but to see him up-close and personal for the first time in ages made her heart race and her cheeks heat. She hoped that as they spent more time together, she'd get over her high school reaction. After all, her schoolgirl crush on him was over. Wasn't it?

She was too old for crushes, darn it. She was just admiring a handsome man. That's all.

At the table, Dustin and Andy were deep

in conversation about bull riders and their statistics. Too bad that Andy didn't pay as much attention to his arithmetic as he did riding percentages.

Jenna smiled as she set the sandwiches down in front of them. "Anyone want anything to drink?"

"Please," Dustin said.

"Please," Andy said, and Jenna figured that if Dustin asked for a glass of fish oil, Andy would want the same. Just looking at Andy, she could see that the boy was under the spell of Dustin Morgan.

Well, Jenna Reed was going to fight her attraction. Her thirtieth birthday was right around the corner, for heaven's sake, and she wasn't going to fall for one guy. It was time for her to live, to explore and to take risks.

But how was she suppose to do that at Tom's ranch?

She set glasses of milk in front of Andy and Dustin. Dustin pulled out a chair for her from his sitting position as best he could. She smiled her thanks and sat down next to him, looked straight into his dark blue eyes and took a long breath.

"I prepared the guest room for you. It has its own bathroom and shower. I thought that would be more convenient." Jenna took a bite of her sandwich, but she was too nervous to eat any more, sitting so close to Dustin and inhaling his musky scent.

"Thank you. I'm dying to take a shower." He turned to Andy. "But I can't yet due to this dang cast. I can only take a bath, and I can't get it wet."

A picture of Dustin naked flashed into her mind, and her throat went dry. She gulped down some milk.

"Jenna, you haven't said much," Dustin said. "We've got some catching up to do. What are you doing these days—are you still based in Phoenix?"

He leaned over the table as if prepared to give her his complete attention. That was another trait of Dustin's that made the females swoon.

"I've been teaching fourth grade. In my spare time—which isn't much—I coach the district's spelling-bee team and debate team."

Dustin took a bite of his sandwich. "That sounds like a full load."

"It keeps me busy," she said.

"So you're teaching the same grade that Andy had trouble with. No wonder Tom asked you to help him out." Dustin ruffled the boy's hair. "So how are you doing with your math and reading, partner?"

Andy shrugged. "Okay, I guess."

"He's doing terrific," Jenna said, handing Andy his napkin so he'd wipe his mouth. "He's made a lot of progress already."

"It's bor-ring," Andy said, resting his cheek on his palm. "Totally bor-ring."

Dustin shrugged. "Well, maybe I could help,"

Andy nodded. "Cool, Uncle Dustin."

It was very nice of him to volunteer to help Andy, but Jenna was a little put out. She was a teacher, for goodness' sake—she could manage herself.

She tried to figure out something else to say. "How are your parents, Dustin? Tom told me that they like Alaska."

"They love it. My father has taken up hunting again, and Mom has a nice circle of friends that she met at church." He met her gaze. "I still miss your parents, Jenna. Your mom and dad were good to me."

Jenna closed her eyes. She could still see the accident, although the police and Tom hadn't let her approach the scene.

Damn that drunk driver.

She blinked back her tears. "There's not a day that goes by that I don't miss them, too."

Dustin cleared his throat. "Well, if you'll both excuse me, I think I need to rest a little. It's been a long trip."

"I'll show you to the guest room," Jenna said.

"I know where it is."

Of course he did. He visited the ranch often.

"Do you need any help?" she asked.

"No."

She frowned. "If you don't need help, then why are you here?"

He raised an eyebrow. "To supervise the ranch operation."

"You're also here to rest and heal."

Obviously, he wasn't the type to be waited on, but if he refused to let anyone help him, then what was she supposed to do?

Jenna followed Dustin into the hallway that led to his room, so Andy wouldn't overhear their discussion.

"Dustin?" she whispered.

He turned and raised an eyebrow.

"I can't understand why you are refusing my help."

"I'm not refusing. I just need to do things for myself."

She rolled her eyes. "But you can't do everything. Admit it."

"Maybe not, but I sure as hell am going to try."

"Why?"

"Because I always have, Jenna. I've always been self-sufficient. I don't know how to be anything else. I've been on my own since I was eighteen. I've had a lot of responsibility. I've seen a lot, done a lot and no one has ever held my hand through my injuries."

She felt a pang of sadness for him, although he didn't seem sorry for himself at all. He didn't have a home to return to in between bull riding events, not really. She knew his parents sold their ranch when Dustin graduated from high school and took off, and they continued to travel in a motor home. Dustin remained in the Tucson area. He didn't have family around. At least she had Tom.

In a way, Dustin had Tom, too.

But still, he needed help, and he was here. So was she.

"I know you want to remain self-sufficient, and I'll let you do that, as long as you don't hurt yourself doing so. How's that?"

He grinned and touched her arm. His hand callused from riding, was warm to the touch.

"It works for me."

"Good," Jenna said, nodding. "Have a good rest."

She returned to the kitchen, and while Andy finished his lunch, Jenna busied herself in the kitchen, thinking of her conversation with Dustin. She washed a handful of dishes and put everything away.

She sighed as remembered that she would have been in Brussels today.

Just as she closed the refrigerator, she heard a crash and a muffled curse.

"Stay here, Andy," Jenna ordered.

She ran to the guest room, where Dustin was on the floor facedown. Turning his head, he looked up at her, then winced in pain. He was wearing only a pair of white boxers.

"Are you okay?" Jenna knelt down on the floor next to him. She touched his shoulder and ran her hand over his arm. His skin was tanned and warm to her touch, his body tight and muscled. "Anything broken?"

"I'm fine," he said quickly. "Just feeling foolish. I tripped."

"Let me help you up, Dustin," Jenna said. "I don't see how you can do it alone."

Dustin shook his head. "Thanks, but there's no way you can lift me. I'm too heavy. Just get that chair over by the desk and hold it still. I'll use that as leverage."

She held the chair in place and watched as Dustin slowly raised himself up from the floor, dragging his cast. She couldn't help noticing the play of arm, shoulder and back muscles as he pivoted onto the bed, tired.

"Let me cover you up," she said.

"Thanks," he said, avoiding her gaze.

"Maybe you'll let me help you more, Dustin. You could have seriously injured yourself."

"I'm fine."

"Blockhead," she muttered under her breath.

"What's that?"

"*Blanket.* I'll get you a blanket."

She found a brightly striped serape and covered Dustin with it, averting her eyes from his too-perfect body and noticing the circles under his eyes instead.

"Are you willing to admit now that you need my help?" she asked.

He chuckled. "Nope."

She shook her head. "You stubborn…um… ah…*bull rider.*"

"Aww…such praise." His eyes were half-shuttered, but she could still see the twinkling blue hue. "You're the best, Jenna. I mean it."

She'd waited years to hear him say that.

"Close those blue eyes, cowboy. We'll talk later."

"Can't wait to catch up. I want to know what you've been doing. I want…to know… all about you."

He was out. Sleeping. And she was walking on sunshine.

Maybe Dustin wasn't Mr. Right. But he might be Mr. Right Now.

So what was she going to do about it?

Chapter Two

As Dustin slept, Jenna spent the afternoon helping Andy with his reading. He was making painfully slow progress, but it was progress just the same. They still had a lot of work to do yet.

"Sound out the word, Andy," she advised. "You'd know the word if you broke it down to smaller words or sounds."

"Cot...ton...wood," he said slowly.

"It's a tree," Dustin said from the doorway.

He was hanging over his crutches and looked more than a little rumpled.

"Hey, Uncle Dustin!" Andy said, his cute little face brimming with happiness. "Did you have a good sleep? Aunt Jenna said that it's important, that you'll get better faster."

"That's just what my doctor said, buckaroo." He smiled at Andy, then turned to Jenna. "I didn't mean to disturb your lesson."

Andy answered instead. "You didn't." He slid his chair away from the kitchen table and looked hopefully at his aunt.

"Can I go now?"

"Finish the paragraph first," Jenna said.

He pulled his chair back and glanced at the page. "The cot-ton-wood tree is found in North America and can live many, many years."

Dustin cleared his throat. "The cottonwood tree is a good, sturdy tree, Andy. We had one on my father's ranch, and he found out that it's been around for four hundred years." He paused. "That's almost as old as your father."

Andy giggled until Jenna thought he was going to fall out of the chair. Then Dustin pointed to the reading workbook and Andy sobered.

"The cottonwood tree is found in North America and can live many, many years," Andy read once again, then turned to her. "Just like Uncle Dustin said."

"I think we can stop for today, Andy," she said with a sigh.

Dustin put a hand on the boy's shoulder. "I saw a basketball hoop hanging from the barn wall. What do you say we shoot some hoops?"

"Awesome!" Andy replied.

"You're going to have to spot me some points," Dustin said.

"Don't do it, Andy," advised Jenna. "Dustin was an awesome basketball player in high school, and an awesome quarterback, besides being a champion rodeo rider."

Dustin raised an eyebrow and looked at her strangely. "So, you remember that much about me from high school?"

"Well, you were Tom's best friend. He always talked about you. Besides, I went to the games. I saw you play." Absolutely she remembered him. Who wouldn't? He'd always been the perfect jock.

Dustin's eyes twinkled and a smile lit his face. He seemed...pleased by her answer.

Then he winked at Jenna, and her mouth went dry. Darn it. One wink from him in her freshman year of high school would have provided her with four years' worth of joy. But they weren't in high school anymore—and she'd have to remember that.

"I want ten points," Andy insisted.

"I'll spot you ten points only, and that's highway robbery," Dustin protested good-naturedly, continuing the banter.

Jenna knew that the big, lanky cowboy would give Andy anything that he wanted. She knew Dustin's generosity from talking to Tom, and it never failed to tweak her when it came to the boy's birthday, just a bit.

It seemed like Dustin always knew the perfect gifts for a growing boy—a dirt bike, a basketball, a bat and glove—whereas she saw to it that he had a supply of nice clothes for school and books befitting his age.

Of course, Andy's excitement and thankful hugs would be for the fun things, rather than the practical, so Jenna was grudgingly glad that Dustin's gifts made Andy happy. Sure, she could have given him toys and such, but he was growing so fast, and needed clothes. Besides, she always felt the need to be his stand-in mother in the place of the ever-unhappy and lethargic Marla who'd *think* about shopping for Andy when school was well underway.

As she put together a lasagna for dinner,

she could hear the easy dialogue between Dustin and Andy through the open window.

"You shoot like a girl," Andy said.

"I'm on crutches, for Pete's sake."

"I want twenty points from you. Twenty. Even though you shoot like a girl, you still can shoot," Andy said.

"No way, kiddo. We settled for ten."

"Hey, we didn't shake on it."

And on and on it went. Jenna slipped the lasagna into the refrigerator and went outside to join them.

"Want to play, Jenna?" Dustin asked when he saw her approach.

"I was just going to watch."

"C'mon and play along with us. You can be on my team," Dustin said.

"That's not fair," Andy whined.

"What if I give you twenty points?" Dustin asked.

"Thirty."

"Done."

Dustin tossed Jenna the ball. She took a shot. Perfect!

"Beginner's luck," she said with a grin. And it *was* beginner's luck. She wasn't much of a jock.

Ironically, as she started making the occasional basket, Dustin began to miss shot after shot. Unless he was letting Andy win.

How sweet of him.

But, she thought wryly, she didn't have to *let* Andy win. She wasn't that great a player, and most of her shots bounced off the rim.

Despite their good-natured fun, she was all-too aware when Dustin took off his shirt and she saw more proof of his strength.

Suddenly, she felt hot, breathless and shocked at her reaction to him. Mercifully, she'd thought to bring out three bottles of water. She grabbed one and took a long draw, desperate to cool herself and calm her racing pulse.

"Break," she yelled, pushing her bangs off her forehead. She handed both of them a bottle of water. "Dustin needs to rest for a while."

Dustin smiled his thanks, gingerly lowered himself onto a bench and took a long drink. Jenna could see his strong neck move as he swallowed.

She took another sip of water. Darn, it was getting hot out here...

Andy cupped his hands around his mouth. "Time's up!"

Dustin stood up with difficulty. When he

got the ball, he passed it to Jenna. She aimed and made the basket.

They gave each other a high five, but then Dustin's fingers curled briefly around hers and an undeniable jolt shot through her body. It was nothing, she told herself.

She was overreacting.

Admittedly, she didn't have much experience with men. She'd been a wallflower in high school, and her current lifestyle didn't allow her much free time to meet anyone. That's why her trip to Europe had meant so much. She'd needed that vacation for more than one reason.

Not only was it going to be a well-deserved vacation, but it would give her the opportunity to meet men.

For someone about to turn thirty, she hadn't dated much at all. In fact, Jenna could count her dates on one hand—none of which resulted in a serious relationship.

As someone who wanted to get married and have a family, in that old-fashioned order, she hadn't exactly had the time or the opportunity to meet many men.

But now she and Dustin were living together, so to speak, and she had the perfect opportunity to find out if she liked him as much as she'd always thought—and heaven knew she'd thought about him a lot throughout the years.

And she certainly wasn't going to think twice about her brother's silly command to stay away from Dustin, issued after her parents died when she was in her teens. Now, she could truthfully say they were acquaintances who only spoke when Tom was there to chaperone, come to think of it.

Dustin's reputation and occupation spoke of experience with women. He'd always been a player, whereas she hadn't even been in the game.

But she could change that. She remembered a magazine that she'd bought and stuck in her suitcase. It had advertised a specific article about how to catch a man and keep him.

Now, where did she put that magazine?

Dustin pretended to drop the ball, letting Andy retrieve it.

But his mind wasn't on basketball. It was on Jenna and the increasingly obvious attraction between them. She'd ignored him in high school, but surprisingly, she was being nice now. And she'd changed so much. She seemed more relaxed and less stressed. He'd never lacked for female companionship, but this one girl from his past still had a hold on him— and she was the only one he could never have.

He couldn't understand why he was noticing everything about her: the way her blond hair glinted in the desert sun. How her tank top lifted just an inch or so, showing a tanned, taut midriff whenever she threw the basketball. How her whole face lit up when she smiled.

Normally it might not be much of a challenge to use their close quarters as an opportunity to finally get her into bed, but she was Tom's baby sister—and she was definitely off-limits. Even though they were the same age, that didn't matter. She'd always be his best friend's younger sister.

But he'd made his promise long ago. Maybe Tom had forgotten his edict by now. He must have, or else why would Tom push him toward recovering at the Bar R when he knew that Jenna would be there?

Dustin remembered back in high school when he'd told Tom that he wanted to date Jenna. Tom had squashed the idea in a hurry.

"Forget it," Tom had said. "Jenna is something special—she's not just another cheerleader. Keep your hands off her. Promise me."

Dustin hoped that everything was cool with Tom. He knew that if he became involved with Jenna—even after all these years—it would be the end of his friendship with Tom.

He couldn't blame Tom—after all, aside from Andy, Jenna was his only family.

It wasn't worth risking Tom's displeasure by dating Jenna, especially when they weren't just friends, but business partners as well. They co-owned several rank bulls and broncs here on the Bar R.

He tried to concentrate on the game, but he missed his shot, and this time it wasn't on purpose. Jenna was just too distracting.

Just then, she tripped on one of his crutches and fell into him. They both toppled into a heap on the blacktop.

"Are you okay, Jenna?" he asked after they both caught their breaths. He slipped a hand under her head to protect it from the hard surface.

"I'm fine. Just feeling a little clumsy."

"These crutches…" he began. "It's my fault."

He continued to look into her eyes, her big, brilliant green eyes. It wouldn't take much to close the distance between them and taste her full lips.

Something nagged at him, but he pushed

it to the back of his mind. All he wanted to savor right now was the unbelievable feeling of holding Jenna in his arms.

"I'm so sorry!" she gasped, leaping to her feet all too soon. "Oh, Dustin! Did I hurt you?"

Actually, it was a little bit of heaven. Her scent, her body close to his, her weight pressing on him. Nice. He didn't give a hoot about the pain that throbbed around his ankle. "I'll live."

"That's the second time you've been on the ground today. You must be—"

"I'm fine," he said. But he wasn't. He had parts that were killing him, and he didn't mean the parts that were in the cast.

"Let me help you," she said, brow furrowed in concern.

"Just hold on to my crutches, and I'll use them to pull myself up."

He did, but it took him four tries.

"Nice job, Andy." He shook the boy's hand, then hobbled over to the porch, and slumped into one of the rocking chairs. Looking down at the jeans he'd cut up to pull over his cast, he decided to get his mind off Jenna and think of something else.

Like his lack of clothes.

"Jenna, I'm going to get a ranch hand to give me a ride to my apartment so I can pick up some clothes and things."

"I'd be glad to drive you to Tubac," she said, taking a sip of water. "I don't mind at all. Besides, Andy and I could both use a change of scenery. How about tomorrow morning?"

Dustin sighed. So much for trying to stay away from her. Still, there was no polite way to refuse. "I'm meeting with the ranch hands at the bunkhouse first thing in the morning. It shouldn't take long. I just want to have a better handle on the workings of Tom's ranch."

"We can go after your meeting," she said.

"That would be great. Thanks."

He was looking forward to the meeting, and as much as it killed him to impose, the ride with Jenna and Andy would give him something else to look forward to in the morning…

The desert morning dawned hot and bright. Dustin washed his hair in the sink and the rest of him as best he could, vowing to rig up something so he could take a shower or a bath. He could already hear Jenna and Andy in the kitchen. The smell of coffee and something cooking, pancakes maybe, drifted in the air, making his stomach growl.

He could get used to this.

It was all so…homey.

He thought of all the buckle bunnies who hung around the rodeos. They were usually heavily made up and wore low-cut and tight-fitting clothes. Jenna wasn't like them at all. With her no-frills beauty and modest clothes, Jenna was more attractive than any woman he'd met on the circuit.

He could get used to this, if he didn't have other, more immediate goals. He needed to get back to riding bulls and win the PBR Finals in Vegas. That was his plan. Not giving in to a flirtation that could only lead to trouble.

Dustin lumbered into the kitchen and took a big whiff. He hadn't had a good breakfast since…well, it had been a while.

"Morning."

"Good morning, Dustin! How did you sleep?" Jenna's smile brightened the room.

"Better than usual. Breakfast smells great."

"After your meeting with the hands, we'll head out to Tubac," Jenna said, placing a steaming mug of coffee and a plate of eggs and pancakes in front of him.

He'd died and gone to heaven.

Breakfast was fun. Jenna steered the conversation in the direction of Theodore Roosevelt and his part in the making of the National Park System.

That must be the topic of Andy's next reading comprehension essay. Jenna impressed him as a great teacher. He wondered why she'd become one.

When he found himself thinking about her far too much, Dustin excused himself and made his way to the bunkhouse to meet the men. All of them were good guys and hard workers, and they obviously kept the ranch running smoothly. The meeting was over in record time.

When he went back up the path to the main house, he noticed that Jenna had moved her forest-green Chevy SUV closer to his route so he didn't have far to walk.

The ride went fast without a lot of traffic on either I-10 or I-19 South. They talked and laughed and, on a couple of occasions, he glanced at Jenna and noticed her looking back at him.

The three of them pulled up to his apartment building almost an hour later.

"Andy, will you hand me my crutches?" Dustin asked. "I'll give those stairs a try."

Jenna sighed loudly. "You're really going to try to climb three floors? Isn't that the reason you're staying at Tom's ranch, so you don't have to make that climb up and down? You can't go up there. It's too soon after surgery."

"I'm not asking you for more help," he replied.

"Just tell me what you need," she said with a hint of impatience in her voice. "And give me the key."

He shook his head. Damn that bull for doing this to him. Scribbling a quick list, he told her where she could find everything.

"I'll owe you a nice night out when this cast is off." He looked deep into her spring-green eyes. "I mean it."

Jenna blushed and laughed. "Promises, promises. Don't worry. I'll remind you."

He heard the hesitation in her voice.

"You won't have to remind me. I won't forget."

And he wouldn't. His promise to Tom didn't mean that they couldn't go out and have a good time.

Right?

* * *

Jenna never expected that Dustin would live above a shop called Tubac Treasures. It was a charming shop, too, painted in bright primary colors, the window filled with all sorts of Western treasures.

"Here's the key to my apartment," Dustin said, handing her a silver key on a PBR key chain. "The entrance is out back."

She didn't mind going up to his apartment. What she did mind was rifling through his belongings. It would be like invading his privacy.

"Would you like to come with me, Andy?" Jenna asked.

"Nah. I'll stay here with Uncle Dustin. I want to hear about his ride on Black Pearl."

"Okay."

Noticing a small key on his key chain, she guessed that it would open his mailbox, so she decided to pick up Dustin's mail on her way upstairs. His box was packed full—junk mail, a couple of magazines and a huge manila envelope from the sports agent who also represented Tom. Jenna knew immediately what the overstuffed envelope meant—fan letters, most of which were probably from women.

Dustin always was a chick magnet.

She would like to think that she was immune to his charms. She could appreciate a good-looking guy as well as anyone, but Dustin Morgan wasn't for her. She didn't want to be another notch on his belt. Besides, they didn't have anything in common except that he rode bulls and she liked to watch bull riding. That was all.

When she slipped the key into his apartment door, it opened immediately. It was so stuffy inside that she searched for the thermostat in the living room and clicked it to Cool.

She looked around and was surprised to see that the apartment was nicely decorated. Could he have done this himself? Or was it the handiwork of a girlfriend?

She froze. Did Dustin have a special woman in his life?

Telling herself it didn't matter—she wasn't interested, remember?—she moved into the bedroom. She didn't know what to expect— mirrors?—but it was neat and clean and conservative. The king bed was covered by a brown plaid comforter. Two dressers made of thick dark wood and a couple of matching nightstands were the only other pieces in the room.

Western art adorned the walls—beautiful ink drawings painted in watercolors. There were pictures of cowboys riding bulls and broncs, old pueblo villages, saguaros, mountains. She was particularly drawn to a beautiful painting of the old San Xavier del Bac Mission, on the outskirts of Tucson. It was perfect in every detail.

The artist was talented—very talented. She squinted to make out the name, but could only see a capital *M*. She'd have to remember to ask Dustin who the artist was. He or she must be in residence in Tubac, and she'd love to invest in some of their work.

Checking her watch, she realized she'd already been in the apartment for ten minutes. Hurrying to his dresser, she pulled open a drawer and grabbed shirts, sweatpants and clean socks and—she tried not to look—underwear, along with a pair of sneakers from the closet. She packed everything inside a duffel bag she'd found on the closet shelf.

She paused to admire the San Xavier painting again, then set the thermostat back to Off and hurried downstairs before she lingered to explore the other bedroom.

She'd learned a lot about Dustin in this trip. He lived alone. He was an art collector. And someone—a girlfriend?—had probably decorated his apartment for him.

Back at the car, she put the duffel bag in the backseat next to Andy and settled back in the driver's seat.

"I can't thank you enough, Jenna," Dustin said.

"No problem." She waved his concern away. "You have a beautiful apartment. Who decorated it for you?"

"I did it myself," he said.

Strike one.

"And you live alone right now?" She knew it wasn't any of her business but she couldn't help herself.

He nodded. "I've always lived by myself."

Strike two.

"And the artist whose paintings you collect…well, he or she is just fabulous. I particularly like the one of San Xavier Mission. It's magnificent."

"Thank you," he said.

She got into the driver's seat. "Could you tell me the name of the artist? I'd like to commission another one."

Dustin laughed. "I don't know if I can tell you the artist's name. He's very exclusive."

"I'd really like to know."

"Okay," he said. "Since you've been so good to me, I'll tell you his name." He winked. "His name is Dustin Morgan."

"What?" She was stunned. "You're the artist?"

"I am."

Strike three.

Dustin Morgan was an artist—an *exceptional* one. Who would have thought?

Chapter Three

Dustin was amazed that Jenna thought so much of his paintings. She was as excited as if she'd just discovered the next da Vinci.

Da Vinci he wasn't.

As far as Dustin was concerned, he didn't want to talk about his art. He wanted to eat. They'd stopped for lunch at a little hole in the wall that had the best Mexican food in all of Arizona.

"I paint for fun, Jenna," he said, hoping that would end the discussion.

She paused from eating her chicken chimichanga. "But you are so talented!"

"I sell my work at the store downstairs from my apartment."

"But you're bigger than Tubac Treasures. I mean, I minored in contemporary art in college, and I can see how good you are."

How could he make her understand how he felt about his art?

"Jenna, my drawing and painting is just a hobby. It's not who I am. I'm a bull rider."

"You're so wrong, Dustin. You're an artist, too."

She didn't get it. Probably because she had always been driven about everything.

From what he'd heard about Jenna throughout the years via Tom, she hadn't changed much. She always thought big and jumped right in to make something happen, whereas he was content just doing what he did—bull riding and watercolors.

He squirted more jalapeño sauce on his tamale. "When it stops being fun and starts becoming work, then that's when I quit."

Andy wiped at his mouth with a handful of napkins. Andy looked like he had more taco on him than he was initially served. "School is work, Uncle Dustin. I want to quit."

Jenna shot Dustin an exasperated look.

"I didn't mean school, Andy. You need to

go to school so you can learn as much as you can and eventually get a good job," Dustin said, hoping he could clarify things.

"I'm going to quit school as soon as I can and be a bull rider like you and Dad and win a lot of money."

Jenna opened her mouth to say something, then shot a pleading look in his direction.

Dustin leaned toward Andy. "I wanted to go to college after high school. I wanted to study business and how to manage animals. It's called animal husbandry. Both of those things are really important when you want to run your own ranch, which I want to do someday."

Andy appeared to be listening, so he continued. "I couldn't go to college because my parents needed help on their ranch. So, I worked at the ranch during the day, rode bulls on the weekend, and went to night school three nights a week."

"When did you study?" Jenna asked.

"Every spare moment I could," Dustin replied. "It wasn't easy, but I wanted something to fall back on when I retired from the sport."

Jenna smiled at him and nodded. "You deserve a lot of credit, Dustin."

"Thanks." He basked in her smile for a

while, they turned to Andy. "And your dad deserves a lot of credit, too, right Andy? I'm sure you know that he's taking classes on-line. True?"

Andy nodded solemnly. He knew when he was outnumbered.

"So, two bull riders in the top ten of the rankings, and your aunt, Jenna, who moved here to help you pass, can't be wrong."

"Oh, okay," Andy said grudgingly, getting up from the table. "Excuse me. I need to use the bathroom."

Jenna nodded. "You're excused."

After Andy left, Jenna shook her head. "Congratulations on getting your degree, Dustin. Now I know why you turned down that scholarship to UNLV. Your parents needed you."

She reached across the table and put her hand over his.

It was an impulsive gesture, but when she didn't move it away, he stroked the top of her hand with his thumb. Her eyes grew as wide as the belt buckle he wore. All too soon, Andy returned from the restroom, and Dustin pulled his hand away.

He shrugged. "I just did what I had to do."

Sometimes he thought it was all for nothing, because all too soon his parents gave up, sold the place and moved on. That had hurt him. He'd loved that ranch and had worked hard alongside his parents so they could keep it in the family. He always thought that his dad had called it quits too soon.

Dustin had hoped to buy back the ranch after he started climbing in the PBR standings, but it had virtually disappeared. A developer subdivided it into housing and a golf course.

Andy joined them in the booth and reached for his soda.

Jenna cleared her throat. "Dustin, speaking of school, have you taken any art classes?"

He grunted. Jenna certainly had a one-track mind.

"No. I haven't, but I've studied Western art on my own."

"Studied on your own? That's really wonderful, Dustin."

Dustin bit back a grin. It figured that Jenna, the eternal bookworm, would be impressed by that.

"Everyone done?" he asked, changing the subject. Inside his cast, his ankle was throbbing and itching. He didn't know how much longer he could endure the damn thing.

Dustin peeled off some bills and dropped them on the table, including a hefty tip for the service. Jenna was digging in her purse for her wallet, but he waved her away. "I got it, Jenna."

She smiled her appreciation. "Next time we all go out, it'll be my treat."

A big hit of pleasure washed over him. He'd like nothing better than to go out with them again. Or even better on a bonafide date with Jenna.

Jenna stood at the kitchen sink peeling potatoes for dinner. Dustin was at the bunkhouse, talking to the ranch hands. Andy was shooting hoops in the yard.

The ride to Tubac had been a welcome change from two weeks of getting Andy up for summer school, tutoring him at night and doing the cooking and cleaning. Until today, she hadn't been off the ranch in a week.

Maybe this weekend, they could go to Old Tucson, visit the movie studio where they made westerns, or even go out for lunch or dinner.

Of course she'd invite Dustin. He had to be bored sitting around most of the day with his ankle up.

Dustin. She was always a little too jumpy with him and felt that she always had to be "on." He made her so nervous—her heart racing, her cheeks heating and her mouth bone dry—that she just couldn't relax and be herself.

She had to forget about him and concentrate on the task at hand—getting Andy up to speed on fourth-grade reading and math. He was making excellent progress, but he wasn't having fun. She'd have to change things up, try something besides his reading workbook. But what would pique his interest? Comic books?

Out of the window, she could see Dustin struggling to walk with his crutches up the narrow path from the bunkhouse on uneven terrain. She really should ask one of the hands to widen the path. It was overgrown with prickly pear cactus and other desert vegetation.

Wiping her hands on a towel, she hurried outside to help Dustin. She didn't want him to fall again. "Maybe we should get a wheelchair for you."

He answered her suggestion with a scowl. "I'm fine, Jenna."

"Well, be careful." His bare toes were inches

away from the sharp needles of a prickly pear cactus.

He followed her gaze. "I know about cacti. I've lived in Arizona all my life."

"So have I," Jenna said firmly. "So don't get stuck."

"I don't need a nurse. I'm a bull rider, for heaven's sake. I can manage a pair of crutches."

"Fact one: I am not a nurse. And fact two: It was that sport that put you in that cast, cowboy. If you can't stand to be helped, then just stay in the guest room and starve to death." Her cheeks heated. "And stop your complaining. You know, I could have been in *Ireland* today, but instead I'm here."

Jenna couldn't believe she'd said that. Turning, she ran down the path, up the porch steps and into the house. Leaning against the back of the door, she caught her breath.

"Why did I say that?" she muttered.

"Say what, Aunt Jenna?" Andy asked from the doorway of the kitchen.

She jumped. The last she knew, Andy was playing basketball.

"It's nothing, sweetie. Go back to your game."

He shrugged and left. Obviously, the explanation wasn't that exciting.

Dustin. She could hear him struggling and

grunting up the steep porch steps. The way he was acting, she should just let him fend for himself.

But she wanted him to get better, so she was going to help him if he liked it or not. Then Mr. *Tough* Cowboy could get back to the *tough* sport of bull riding and out of her hair.

Complaining? He wasn't *complaining.* If anything, he was just stating fact.

Dustin vowed to be more appreciative of Jenna's help. He just wasn't a good patient—he preferred to take care of himself.

But what did Jenna mean about Ireland?

As he struggled up the steps to the porch, he tried to remember what she'd said.

I could have been in Ireland today.

She wouldn't have given up a trip to Ireland to take care of him, would she? Nah. She really didn't even know him, and throughout the years, she'd barely spoken to him.

If she gave up a trip for anyone, it would have been for Andy.

He planned on getting Jenna alone and asking her to clarify what she'd meant.

Andy ran up the porch steps. "Uncle Dustin, what are you going to do now?"

"I think I'll talk to your Aunt Jenna for a while."

"Do you wanna shoot some hoops?" Andy asked.

"I'll play with you later tonight. Deal?"

Andy burst into a big grin, then it faded as his shoulders slumped. "I forgot. I have to be tutored tonight."

"Maybe, if things go well with your tutoring, it won't take that long, and we can play. Cool?"

"Awesome."

They bumped knuckles, and Andy leaped off the stairs and was gone.

He'd love to be that young and agile again. Recently, he'd been thinking of hanging up his spurs and settling down—after he won the finals in Vegas, of course. He wanted a ranch like the Bar R and a wife to share it with. Maybe even a couple of kids.

Dustin sighed. Here he was only thirty, and he was thinking about his life like an old man. The best was yet to come, but it wouldn't—couldn't—be as a bull rider. Bull riders had short careers. There weren't many still riding over the age of thirty-five.

He caught a glimpse of Jenna through the front window, reading a magazine in the living room. He could almost picture walking through the door after a hard day's work and being welcomed home by her. They'd kiss and talk about their day. Their children would be totally loved, perfectly behaved and their report cards would contain all A's.

And later, at night, he and his wife would make love.

Jenna swung the front door open, pulling him out of his daydream. "Don't worry. I'm not opening the door for you, I just wanted to get some fresh air." She left the door open and went by him in a blur, leaping off the steps of the porch just like Andy had.

Must be a Reed trait.

Dustin would give anything to jump those stairs and follow her.

Instead, he walked into the empty house and wondered if his dreams of a gold buckle, marriage and a family would ever come true. Because regardless of his dreams, he couldn't have Jenna.

Jenna was in the kitchen helping Andy with decimals when she heard a loud thump along with the granddaddy of all curses. Dustin had fallen again.

Her first thought was to rush to help him,

but knowing that her assistance wasn't welcome, she forced herself to concentrate on her nephew and his fourth-grade math.

"I think Uncle Dustin fell. Aren't we going to help him up, Aunt Jenna?"

"If Dustin needed our help, he'd give a yell."

"He did yell. He yelled fu—"

"Andrew Reed!"

"Oh, all right. I wasn't going to say it."

"And Dustin shouldn't have said it, either. I'm going to have a talk with him." As she got up stiffly from her chair, she knew that she sounded like the teacher that she was, and Dustin was about to experience her wrath— just like one of her students would.

She found him in the living room, sitting on the couch. When Dustin saw her standing there, he hurried to explain.

"I was trying to get the remote from on top of the TV," he said. "It was just out of my reach, and I lost my balance with this damn cast. I used the crutches for leverage to get to the couch."

"Dustin," she said firmly. "Your language—"

"Sorry. If I offended you, I apologize."

She nodded, noticing how pale he was from

the exertion, and the awkward angle of his bad leg.

"I'd offer to try and make you more comfortable, but I know how much you want to do things on your own," she said, feeling that they'd had this discussion before.

He just sat there with his arms folded, looking...frustrated.

"I'm getting too weak, sitting all day. I need to lift weights or something," he said. "I'm not used to just sitting around, and I shouldn't take it out on you."

Jenna didn't move.

"So...thanks." Dustin looked up at her. "Why don't you get back to your lesson?"

Obviously, he was embarrassed. But his apology—for both his profanity and his rejection of her—was sincere. Maybe, finally, she could try to figure him out.

Jenna went to the door and called Andy in from the kitchen. "Andy, take a break. Shoot some hoops if you want. I'll give you a call when we're going to start again."

Andy hesitated. The sweet kid wanted to lend a hand. Jenna waved him away. "Go ahead."

Andy hurried out the door, and Jenna took a seat on the rocker.

"Okay, cowboy. Now that I have your un-divided attention, please explain why it's so hard for you to accept any help from me."

Several seconds went by before he spoke. "I've always done things by myself. It's as simple as that. It's not you, Jenna, although I don't want to impose on you anymore than I already have. I truly appreciate everything you're doing for me."

Dustin leaned back into the sofa cushions. "Every time I've been injured, I've managed by myself. I live alone. I can't count on any-one being there every time. Besides, I'm a big, tough cowboy." He leaned toward her. "But getting to know you again is an extra bonus."

Jenna's heart soared. She looked at his sky-blue eyes, his smile that seemed sin-cere. "Thanks. I feel the same way about you, but—"

Dustin chuckled. "I knew there'd be a *but*."

"*But,* I think you're wrong about accept-ing help. I get where you're coming from, though."

He raised an eyebrow. "Anything else you'd like to know?"

"Are you involved with someone?" she

blurted, then took a deep breath. Could she be any more obvious?

"No. I'm not."

She sat back in her chair, relieved. So, he was fair game.

"What about you, Jenna? Do you have a boyfriend lurking in the cacti? A passel of children somewhere?"

She grinned. "No children. No husband." Her smile faded a little. "My students are my children. I mean… I would have liked children of my own, but it didn't happen. Now, I'm moving on. I've cut down on my hours and I promised myself that I'm going to travel more. No moss will grow under these…flip-flops."

He was quiet for a while, studying her. Jenna felt that she'd disappointed him somehow. She decided to change the subject.

"You know, Dustin, I've been wanting to ask you something else."

"Shoot."

"Did you save your parents' ranch?"

Dustin nodded. "For a while. Then they got an offer they couldn't refuse and sold out and bought a place in Florida. Now they're in Alaska." He looked down at the carpeted floor. "They gave me some of the money from the sale, which I've invested in rough stock here at Tom's ranch." He lowered his voice, as if thinking out loud. "When I win the finals, I'll buy my own ranch. And someday, I'll have a bunch of children who I'll teach to rope and ride and…"

He stopped and looked deep into her eyes. "So, now you see, Jenna—" Dustin lifted the bad leg and stretched it out in front of him. "I had no choice but to turn down that scholarship."

"I admire you, Dustin. I do. And you even found time to get your bachelor's degree."

He smiled. "And don't forget my master's."

She stared at him, willing her brain to wrap around what he'd just said. Finally, it sank in. He had a master's degree, and he was riding bulls?

"Really?" Jenna stopped rocking and leaned forward. "What's your master's in?"

"Business. And my bachelor's degree is in animal husbandry." He grinned. "Tom and I will take the rodeo world by storm by breeding a new generation of bulls and broncs."

She couldn't help but be impressed. Dustin was certainly a self-made man, and she just knew that his dreams—including those of a ranch and children—would come to fruition.

While her dreams would have to wait. Again.

"Jenna, there's something I've been meaning to ask you, too."

"Shoot," she echoed.

"What did you mean when you said you could have been in Ireland today?"

She was quiet for a moment. "I canceled a three-week trip to Europe because Tom asked me to help Andy pass fourth grade." She sighed. "I would have been having dinner in Dublin tonight."

"Did Tom know about your trip?"

She nodded. "I shouldn't have told him. He would have made other plans, but I insisted on helping Andy."

"And then you got stuck with me, too."

She held up a warning finger. "I didn't *get stuck* with Andy or you. My trip will be rescheduled."

She remembered that her plan was to have a whirlwind fling with a sexy European. But now Dustin, the man she'd always longed for from afar, was sitting across from her, making her pulse race.

"Andy needed me. Tom needed me. And you need me more than you know," she said.

"You're wrong, Jenna. I know exactly how much I need you." Leaning forward, he issued those two small sentences with great intensity and seriousness.

What he said, how he said it and the expression on his face took her breath away, and she doubted very much that they were talking about his ankle.

Now that she knew Dustin was interested and available, her new plan was to have a fling with a sexy American cowboy.

Chapter Four

The next day, Jenna tried to concentrate on the biography she was reading, but she couldn't. Instead she looked out the window and saw Dustin talking to Adriano, one of the ranch hands. Dustin and he were in an animated discussion, no doubt talking about their greatest bull rides.

She studied Dustin's profile—his square jaw, the hint of a beard, twinkling blue eyes, his perfect nose and lips.

His sensuous lips.

They made her think yet again of the crush she'd had on him in high school. How many times had she doodled their initials in a heart with an arrow through it?

She'd been to every football and basketball game and rodeo event that he'd played in their first two years of high school. She'd been desperate to try and get his attention, but it was nothing more than unrequited love.

She couldn't have been more socially awkward back then. Books were her salvation, and her curse. Her mother always remarked that she should get out more, go to dances and the like, but she hadn't wanted to see Dustin out with other girls.

But now she was too old for crushes. Even though she'd wanted to get married back then—to Dustin—that wasn't the case anymore. She'd decided a while ago that a fling was the way to go.

If she'd gone to Europe, would she have met several men by now? Indulged in some harmless flirting, and then continued on her trip?

But she didn't know how to flirt. Not really. She could recite the periodic tables and calculate pi to the nth degree, but she didn't know how to seduce a man.

Yet here in front of her was a very eligible,

sexy man. Just being around him had heightened every nerve in her body. Trouble was, he was treating her more like a sister than a potential lover, except for a couple of flirtatious comments and absentminded touches.

Could she seduce Dustin?

Her heart beat wildly and her mouth went dry as a plan began to formulate in her mind.

Jenna once again thought of the magazine she'd bought back in Phoenix, just for the article entitled "Ten Ways to Seduce a Man."

She'd thought that the article would help her get a jump start on her goal of seducing a man in Europe. Now, she had another plan.

She knew that she was knowledgeable when it came to academics, but she was totally lacking in whatever she needed to seduce a man—especially a man like Dustin. A man who was right here, right now.

The magazine was still in her suitcase, and she hurried to her bedroom to retrieve it. *Women's Universe* was glossy and slick, loaded with pictures of celebrities and self-improvement articles.

Sitting on the bed, she opened the magazine, turning to page thirty as indicated on the front cover.

She'd read the narrative later. For now,

she'd just skim the highlights. The list of tips for catching a man's eye by dressing—and acting—sexy or confident seemed practical yet…daunting. Wearing lots of makeup, leaving her hair loose and wild had never been her style.

But who was she to argue with *Woman's Universe?*

Well, there was no time like the present to give it her best shot. She tossed the magazine aside and hurried to her closet.

She slipped off her T-shirt and put on the turquoise peasant blouse she'd bought for her vacation, arranging it so it would drape off her shoulder.

Bending over, she flipped her hair forward and brushed it out. Then she tossed her head back and shook it, giving her hair an instant wind-blown look. Then she touched up her makeup, adding lip gloss and blush.

Smoothing down her khaki shorts, she looked at herself in the mirror. Okay, it wasn't her usual style, but she looked pretty good. Confident that she'd done the best she could, she headed out to dazzle Dustin.

She couldn't wait to see his reaction to tips one, two and seven.

* * *

Dustin limped over to where Andy was playing basketball.

"How about some more one-on-one?" Dustin asked.

Andy's face lit up, then slowly dimmed. "I can't. I have to do homework."

"Aunt Jenna's working you hard, huh?"

He shrugged. "It's boring."

"Can I help? I'd be glad to."

"You'll help me?" Andy took off at a run. "Wait there. I'll be right back," he yelled over his shoulder.

Dustin sat down at the patio table. He didn't have to wait long before Andy came racing back, a backpack dangling from his hand.

"It's math homework. I have to do page fifteen and sixteen about decimals." Andy rolled his eyes. "What do I need decimals for?"

"To figure out your money, for one thing."

Andy pointed to the worksheet in the book. It was pretty dry, just rows and rows of addition and subtraction. The next page was multiplication and division.

"Let's look at the first problem. Imagine we're watching bull riding. I rode seven point two seconds. Your dad rode six point nine six seconds. How much time did we ride in total?"

Andy's pencil scribbled. "Fourteen point sixteen seconds," he said quickly.

"What was our average score?" Dustin asked.

"Hey, that's not in the book!"

Dustin chuckled. "Just tell me. I know you can do it."

"Seven point zero eight." Andy grinned.

"Easy, huh? Let's do another one."

And they did. One after another. They did the average NASCAR miles. The division of miles per hour of three racers. More bull riding. And football players gaining yardage.

Jenna appeared after another bull-riding problem. At least he thought it was Jenna. She looked…different. Her hair was loose and she was wearing a lot of makeup. He wondered if she was going out somewhere, and his heart sank as he speculated that she was going on a date. But she would have asked him to watch Andy, so that couldn't be it.

Dustin forced himself to concentrate on helping the boy. He seemed to be learning, so he was going to keep presenting various scenarios. "Three bull riders belonging to the Young Guns team rode a total of 366.75 points. Average their score because the announcer wants to let everyone know on the air," Dustin said, glancing at Jenna.

"Whoa!" Jenna had her hands on her hips. "You were supposed to do your homework on your own, young man."

"But Uncle Dustin is making it fun!" Andy said, looking up from writing his answer. His mouth gaped open as he pointed at Jenna. "Hey, Aunt Jenna, why are you so dressed up?"

Swallowing, she patted her hair and tucked in a bra strap "I—I—um…"

A light breeze carried the scent of her perfume toward Dustin. Roses.

"I'm sorry that I interfered, Jenna," he said sincerely. "I had asked Andy if he wanted to shoot hoops, but when he said he had homework, I thought I'd help. Blame me."

Jenna held up a finger, telling him to wait, and smiled woodenly at Andy, who still looked at her like she'd just dropped in from another planet. "Andrew Reed, please go into the house and finish your homework on your own. Okay?"

"Yeah."

When Andy was out of hearing range, Jenna turned to Dustin. "I'm not blaming you. And if Andy is learning by your method, then that's perfectly fine with me."

Actually, it sounded as if she were annoyed—and he decided to call her on it. "You don't sound perfectly fine. You sound mad."

She fussed with the hem of her blouse. "I'm mad at myself. I should have taught Andy using sports examples like you did. Math can be dull to a kid. You made it come alive. I just bored him to death with the standard textbook because I was so focused on catching him up with the rest of his class."

He studied her spring-green eyes, now surrounded by blue eye shadow. "Don't be too hard on yourself, Jenna. Not every problem on every test is going to have a story about bull riding or car racing on it."

She tugged on her blouse again. Her bra strap peeked out, and she impatiently tucked it back in. He'd never seen anyone fight with a bra and a blouse so much.

"Just wait until I use the amount of manure a bull can produce when Andy has to learn square feet and cubic feet," Dustin said, grinning.

Jenna laughed. He loved the sound of it, and wished that she'd do it more often. She was way too serious.

He tried not to look, but her hair was sticking out in several places. She nervously tucked it behind her ear. Better.

Dustin didn't know what her new hairstyle was all about, or what was up with her choice of blouse, but he'd figure it out sooner or later.

To be honest, he didn't know if he liked her new look. She was always fresh-faced, her hair tucked into a ponytail, with a dusting of freckles on her nose and a bright smile. Right now, she looked like some of the buckle bunnies that followed him and the other riders.

He had to admit that he liked the fact that the gauzy blouse revealed a little more skin. Hell, he'd always thought that she was an attractive woman, but now…well, she just didn't look like the Jenna he'd always known. The woman he'd always wanted.

His cell phone rang. He answered the call, making a gesture of apology to Jenna.

"Hey, Jeff," he said, greeting his agent. "I'm doing okay."

There was some idle chitchat about the weather before Jeff got around to the purpose of his call.

"Remember that commercial for Scents of the West—the one for the men's aftershave called Eight-Second Ride? Anyway, the film crew is coming out to Tom's ranch to shoot the commercial with you in it. They know you have a cast on your ankle, but they'll work around the thing."

Dustin didn't like this part of being on top of the standings, but he owed it to his sponsor to support their products.

"When?" he asked.

"Tomorrow, if you're up to it."

"I'm doing okay. What time?"

"First thing in the morning."

He had planned on hitching a ride with one of the hands to check on the progress of the fence mending on the border of the south pasture. Then he'd wanted to update himself on the breeding and birthing records of the rough stock.

All that would have to wait until after the commercial. He certainly couldn't turn down the cash.

"I'll be ready," Dustin said. He disconnected the call and went into the house to tell Jenna about the taping. He wasn't sure how she would feel about yet another disruption that would distract Andy.

Letting himself into the living room just as it started to rain, he found Jenna sitting on the sofa watching a game show on TV.

He hung his wet hat on the rack behind the door and sat down on a side chair.

"Uh… Jenna. I have something to tell you."

She raised an eyebrow. "Okay," she said cautiously.

"A film crew is coming here to shoot a commercial tomorrow morning. Early."

"Oh?"

"I'm in it. It's something my agent dreamed up for publicity. I hope you don't mind."

"I don't mind a bit. It sounds exciting," she said, wetting her lips.

It was an insignificant gesture, but it immediately got him thinking of hot, wet kisses and a soft, warm mattress…and Jenna.

He started to tweak his hat to her, but remembered he'd hung it by the door. "See you later."

He hurried to the kitchen. Noticing a magazine ruffling in the breeze from the open window, he thought he'd read it to take his mind off Jenna.

When he saw it was *Woman's Universe,* he tossed it back on the table.

Then his eyes caught the heading in blazing

orange letters: TEN WAYS TO SEDUCE A MAN. Curious, he turned to the story. Skimming the article, he smiled, then sobered. Like the burn of cheap whiskey, a shot of jealousy ran through him. What guy was she thinking of seducing when she was doing her hair and putting on sexy clothes and perfume? Was he a neighboring rancher, or someone she taught school with?

He inhaled and closed his eyes to clear his head. It shouldn't matter what she did. She was off-limits. He shouldn't care.

But he did.

Breakfast with Jenna the next day was very awkward. It was just the two of them, as Andy had already left on the bus for summer school.

Jenna's hair looked like she'd just walked out of a wind tunnel, and she kept staring at him and asking him a million questions.

He still wanted to know who was the lucky object of the "Ten Ways to Seduce a Man" article—and why she thought she needed a magazine to teach her how to lure a man. Didn't she realized how attractive she was?

Right now, he felt like he was going through

a police interrogation with all the questions she was asking him.

But when she got him to talk about bull riding, he was off and running.

"What bull do you like to ride the best?" she asked, leaning closer to him, her green eyes intent.

"Black Pearl," he replied, taking a sip of coffee. Once again, he was struck by how different she looked with full makeup—and by a longing for her more simple, straightforward look. The look of the girl he'd always wanted.

Then, as he leaned back in his chair, he spotted her legs—her tanned, crossed legs. On the tips of her ruby-red polished toes dangled a blue flip-flop. She was swaying it back and forth.

He'd never thought that a blue flip-flop was sexy, but now he watched, hypnotized by the movement of her calf muscles and her knee as she swayed the rubber sandal.

It hit the floor, and he was at the ready to retrieve it and slip it back on her foot as if she were Cinderella at the ball.

But she slipped her foot into the flip-flop again and returned it to the dangling position.

Damn that magazine article!

When he finally looked up, she met his gaze with a smile. She knew exactly what effect she was having on him.

"So what's it like to have a whole gaggle of buckle bunnies after you?" she asked.

"I don't have a gaggle," he said trying to concentrate on answering the question but dying to look at her legs again.

"I've seen them buzzing around you, just like the girls, in high school. You've never lacked for female companionship, have you?" she asked.

He shrugged. How could he answer that without sounding conceited?

Sway...sway...

She raised an eyebrow. "You were always surrounded by cheerleaders and every cute girl within a fifty-five mile radius."

But it was you I wanted.

He chuckled. "I think you're exaggerating."

"Not by much, Dustin, and you know it. You were voted King of the senior prom. And you took the head cheerleader."

"Karen McArtle asked *me* to go with *her* to the prom."

He barely could remember Karen's face. In fact, he'd only accepted to see Jenna all dressed up. She didn't have an actual date. She just went with her friends from the debate club.

He took another sip of coffee so he didn't have to look at Jenna's green eyes

Can't look at her eyes. Can't look at her legs.

He'd wanted to ask her to the senior prom, but he hadn't dared. For one thing, Tom wouldn't have liked it, and Jenna showed absolutely no interest in him. Besides, he didn't think he could have handled a rejection from her, not with all the pressure he was under at the time to help his parents.

"Did you enjoy yourself at the prom?" he found himself asking.

She looked as shocked as he felt for asking such a dumb question after all these years.

"I can't remember," she said, brows furrowed. "It was so long ago."

"I wanted to ask you to dance," he blurted. But he hadn't. The darn promise he'd made to her brother stopped him cold.

Her eyes widened in surprise. "You did?"

"I did."

She tilted her head, and suddenly he couldn't take his eyes off her lush lips. "Then why didn't you?"

He shrugged. "You were busy with your friends."

"I would have danced with you, Dustin," she said softly.

His mouth went dry, and it was hard for him to form a response, but he tried to be casual. "Yeah?"

She blushed. "Sure."

Double damn. All that night he'd debated and warred with himself, only to discover years later he could have held Jenna in his arms. How many other opportunities had he missed out on? Was this summer his chance to finally let her know how he'd always felt about her?

I wanted to ask you to dance.

Jenna picked up the dishes and flip-flopped her way to the sink. She hated the darn things. She'd only brought them to wear around the pool.

But they'd worked well enough. She smiled as she loaded the dishwasher. Dustin couldn't take his eyes off her legs.

Clearly *Women's Universe* knew their stuff!

And she'd lied to him about the senior prom, she thought with a rush of guilt. She remembered that night vividly, but she couldn't admit that to him.

How she'd wanted to ask Dustin to take her! But what could she do? The day she worked up enough courage to ask *him,* Tom mentioned that Dustin was out of town with the rodeo. When her courage vanished, there he was, hanging out with her brother at their house.

As she put soap into the dishwasher, she flashed back to Dustin walking into the gym with Karen. She'd almost burst into tears. Dustin looked so handsome in his black tux, flashing a contented smile. She got through that evening by avoiding him.

Why the hell hadn't he asked her to dance?

Her face heated as she thought about dancing with Dustin. That would have made the evening special. Instead, she cried herself to sleep that night, feeling alone and unwanted.

It was hard being a geek in high school. All the boys wanted cheerleaders, or bubbly, social, popular girls. Smart, bookish girls usually went without dates.

She slammed the dishwasher shut and turned it on.

"Thanks for breakfast, Jenna. I appreciate it."

"You're welcome."

"Well," he sighed, "I'd better get ready to greet the film crew." He got his crutches and walked out of the kitchen.

She wiped off the table, tossed the cloth into the sink and sat back down.

She wanted him. More than ever.

She knew now that Dustin was not immune to the Ten Ways.

He obviously thought that big hair and a dangling flip-flop were turn-ons.

Well, that was nothing. She had a few tips left to try, and she was going to go all out.

Dustin was doing a slow burn. He was getting all worked up over a woman he'd sworn to stay away from.

The doorbell rang and Dustin was glad for something to take his mind off of Jenna. "I'll get it," he yelled in the direction of the kitchen. "It's probably the crew."

"Okay."

Shaking all their hands, he invited them in, and introductions were made—the director, the makeup artist, lighting director, assistant to the director and two interns.

"Can we see the pool area?" asked the director, Skip, a tall, thin man with a red cowboy hat that seemed too big for him. He sported a red bandanna around his neck.

"This way," Dustin said, motioning with his head.

On the way to the pool, he introduced them to Jenna, who was reading the paper in the kitchen.

"They'd like to see the pool," he explained to her.

She nodded. "Sure."

"Come with us," Dustin said. He wanted her to be there. After all, this was her brother's house, and it was her solitude they were all disturbing.

They walked through the sliding glass door and fanned out on the concrete patio of the rectangular pool.

"Looks perfect," Skip said, turning to Dustin. "But we have a problem. Just as I pulled into your driveway I received a call that the actress that we were going to use had an allergic reaction to a bee sting. She's out. I'll have to call for another. Or we could just shoot you alone, but then we're going to have to come up with another script. So it might take longer then we thought. We might have to stay overnight—in a hotel, of course."

Dustin didn't relish dragging this out or

being in the desert sun with a sweaty cast on for any length of time. Besides, there was a beautiful woman right here who could fill in perfectly.

"How about Jenna?" Dustin asked.

Chapter Five

Dustin watched as six pairs of eyes looked at him, then shifted right to Jenna. She looked shocked, then her cheeks heated into two pink stains.

"Oh, I couldn't," she protested softly.

The director rubbed his chin. "What do you think, Leslie?"

Leslie was the makeup artist. She walked over to Jenna and studied her face, touched her hair, made her turn around twice.

Jenna rolled her eyes. "I can't. I—"

"Her hair is a disaster right now," Leslie proclaimed. "But I can work with it."

"Jenna?" Dustin asked. He wasn't beneath

pleading. He was uncomfortable doing this kind of thing and wanted to get it over with. Besides, doing the commercial with Jenna would be more fun. "Would you mind helping out?"

"I'm not an actress. I'm a fourth-grade teacher."

"You'll be perfect. And the sooner this shoot is finished, the sooner we can get back to normal around here," Dustin said. "Whatever *normal* is."

"Look, Jenna." Skip, the director, put his arm around her, and Dustin clenched his fists. "Dustin is the focus of this commercial. You just have to walk on and hug him. You don't have to do any lines. That's it."

Jenna looked apprehensive. Then her lips softened into a nervous smile. "I'll be glad to fill in."

Skip clapped his hands. "Terrific! Let's get to work, people."

Jenna sat on the edge of the tub in the master bathroom, watching as Leslie lugged in what looked like a canister vacuum cleaner. "Where can I spray-tan you, Jenna?"

"Spray-tan?" Jenna started to laugh but bit it back. She didn't want to hurt Leslie's feelings. "In the shower, I guess," she said, praying that it would wash off if it got on the tiles.

After Leslie got set up, she instructed Jenna to go into the shower with just her bra and panties on. "Wear something that you don't mind throwing away," she suggested.

She didn't mind throwing away any of the underwear she'd brought with her to the Bar R. It was just utilitarian, not the fancy stuff that she'd bought for her trip to Europe.

Leslie handed her a shower cap and a pair of goggles. "Ready?"

"As I'll ever be," Jenna replied.

The spray was cool at first; but then she got used to it. "Turn around slowly," Leslie said. She turned, feeling like a chicken on a rotisserie.

After that was over, Jenna's hair was washed, conditioned, blow-dried and baked with a curling iron. It had more product on it than the shelves of the corner drugstore carried. But Leslie truly created magic. It looked sleek and sexy, with a lot of bounce and it was the best-looking hairstyle of her life.

Her finger and toenails were cut, polished and buffed until they gleamed. Her makeup took forever—it felt as if every pore was filled with a different kind of cream or powder. But at last she was done, and turned to the mirror for a look.

Wow. She didn't even recognize herself.

She couldn't wait to see Dustin. Wouldn't he be surprised?

Leslie left the room but soon returned holding up two strips of colorful material.

"What's that?" Jenna asked.

"Your costume," Leslie replied.

Jenna swallowed hard. "What is it supposed to be?"

"A bikini."

"I see…a bikini for a men's aftershave commercial." Jenna sniffed. Actually, she didn't see, but she understood. "Bring it on." They both laughed.

Jenna took the bathing suit from Leslie and fingered the shiny material. "I hope it fits."

"We can alter it somewhat," Leslie added with a grin.

"Can you add a yard of material to it?" she said, slipping into the suit.

A knock on the door halted their laughter. "Are you about ready?" Skip yelled. "I don't want to lose the light."

Jenna looked at herself in the mirror and couldn't believe that the suit was actually flattering. Oh, she could stand to lose ten pounds or so, but she filled out the suit nicely.

"You're a magician, Leslie. I look…well, I don't look like myself."

Leslie put a hand on her shoulder. "You look gorgeous. I just enhanced what was already there."

She put on a bathrobe and nodded to Leslie, and they both left the bedroom.

A shot of excitement ran through her when she thought of Dustin's reaction to her look.

When Jenna returned, Dustin couldn't take his eyes off her. Her blond hair shimmered in the sun and curled softly around her face. Whatever makeup she had on brought out her green eyes.

She looked like the Jenna he'd always preferred—wholesome yet sexy at the same time. Her eyes twinkled either in amusement or in anticipation of acting in a commercial.

Then she slid off the bathrobe she was wearing, and his jaw dropped.

She wore a bikini with stripes of primary colors slashed across the strips of fabric. On her feet were her blue flip-flops, which matched the skimpy suit perfectly. Gold jewelry glistened around her neck and an ankle and dangled from her ears.

"Jenna?" he croaked. The fourth-grade teacher looked like a swimsuit model.

"Of course." She laughed and shifted on her feet. He noticed how long and shapely her legs were.

He couldn't swallow over the lump stuck in his throat.

"You look...wonderful," he finally said, thinking that Jenna didn't need "Ten Ways to Seduce a Man." She just had to show up dressed like this.

"Thanks."

But he'd liked her before, too—the Jenna who somehow twisted her blond hair and clipped it back with a barrette. The Jenna who wore cutoff jeans and a T-shirt to play hoops. The Jenna he'd see helping Andy with his reading or math, who was so patient and kind with the boy.

This Jenna was different. This Jenna crossed her long legs and dangled a blue flip-flop and aroused him more than any woman ever had.

She was hypnotic.

"Remember, we can only shoot Dustin from the thighs up," Skip announced. "I'm going to make it seem like he's sitting in a chair by the pool and taking in the sun and scenery. Jenna, you're the scenery."

She laughed. "I've never been called scenery before."

"Dustin, take your shirt off," ordered Skip. "You're lounging by the pool, not sitting in the chutes at a rodeo."

"Let's get this over with," Dustin mumbled.

Jenna smiled. "What would you like me to do, Skip?"

"I want you to walk toward Dustin and give him a secret smile, like you know something and he doesn't. When you get to him, wrap your arms around his neck and put your cheek against his."

The camera crew helped Dustin into a chair and checked the lighting, and there he sat, waiting.

As Jenna moseyed toward him, Dustin's mouth went dry. Soon her arms slipped around his neck. He could smell her skin and feel the softness of her cheek against his. And felt his promise to Tom become that much harder to keep.

He pushed his hat back and raked his hair with his fingers.

Skip grinned. "That was perfect, Jenna.

But Dustin, you looked uncomfortable." He shook his head. "I need you to be in the moment. Let's try it again. But this time, I'd like you both to get close so that your lips are almost touching, but not quite."

Dustin waited in anticipation of Jenna's arms going around him. He groaned when he realized that he'd thought that this would be fun. Instead it was pure torture.

What would Tom say about the commercial when it was released?

Maybe nothing. After all, it was just a little commercial. It didn't mean anything. He'd dreamed of being close to Jenna many times before, but just like then, this wasn't real. It was just acting.

Dustin looked into Jenna's eyes as if he were paralyzed. It seemed like it took hours for him to move close to her, to position his lips close to hers.

Dustin could hear the soft intake of Jenna's breath, and his heart beat faster. This was Jenna, the woman of his high school dreams, the woman who was always forbidden to him, the woman he admired from afar.

He got lost in the green depths of her eyes and then, in spite of Skip's direction to the contrary, his lips touched hers.

* * *

Dustin was kissing her!

Jenna tried not to react, to play it cool and act like his soft, sweet kiss didn't faze her in the least.

But her knees just wouldn't lock in place, and her heart was dancing wildly in her chest. Her face was so hot, she was sure that it would appear flaming red on film.

She slowly moved away from him surprised to see that he looked as shocked as she felt. Then he broke into a sly grin, the same grin that had charmed many a high school girl and scores of buckle bunnies. That Dustin Morgan grin was a killer, both boyishly charming and highly masculine at the same time.

He must be playing with her. Well, maybe the kiss didn't mean a thing to him, but it meant everything to her.

"Cut!" shouted Skip. "I like the kiss. It works. Dustin, put more passion into it. Everyone, let's take it from the top again and really give me passion."

Jenna tried to feel confident as she pasted on what she thought was a sexy smile. Her heart pounded as she slipped her arms around Dustin and ran her hands down the smoothness of his chest, then his arms. Jenna had always known that his arms would be thick with muscles and sinew, but she wasn't prepared for the rush of excitement that vibrated through her body at the feel of her skin against his.

She didn't know what had made her touch Dustin in such a way, but she figured that she might as well make the most of this opportunity. When the film crew left, it would be back to normal for them both—Jenna longing for Dustin, and Dustin treating her like a sister.

She watched as a smile teased his lips, but it wasn't his usual easygoing grin. Then Dustin's lips covered hers, lightly at first, then harder and more demanding.

Too soon, the kiss was over, and Jenna couldn't move, couldn't think. All she could do was remember that the camera was still on them. Excitement shot through her like a jolt of electricity, hot and shocking.

Dustin ran a finger down her cheek. They both leaned toward each other, touching foreheads, waiting for one of them to react. It was as if she couldn't believe what had just happened and neither could he.

"Cut!" yelled Skip. "That was terrific!" He

turned toward the cameraman. "Tell me that we got that, kid."

"Got it, boss," said the cameraman.

"We'll add the voice-over in the studio," Skip said, checking his watch. "I can't believe how quick that was. Great acting! You should be a professional, Jenna. Any time you want a job, just call me."

I wasn't acting, Jenna thought.

She tried to reestablish eye contact with Dustin, but he was buttoning his shirt.

No matter what, Jenna knew that she'd never forget this day. The way he'd just kissed her...well, he was the one who should become an actor, because he'd almost had her fooled into thinking that he wanted her.

"I'll show you the way out, Skip," Dustin said, walking him toward the kitchen door.

As soon as they all left, Jenna eyed the pool. She wanted to go in—it had gotten pretty hot—but then her makeup would be gone along with her great hairdo. She wasn't ready to stop being Cinderella at the ball.

Then she sighed. Why should the hair and makeup matter when Dustin was just acting?

She walked to the diving board, hopped up, took four quick steps and did a perfect jack-knife into the pool.

As she surfaced and began doing laps, she remembered how he'd bent his head toward hers and they touched foreheads. Was he as unaffected by the moment as she thought?

Hmm… She didn't have much experience in seduction, but even she could tell that he'd felt a spark, too.

Now she had to figure out how to turn it into an inferno.…

Dustin couldn't wait until Skip and his crew were gone.

He'd certainly made a mess of things with Jenna.

He could attribute the first kiss to the fact that a beautiful woman was only inches away from him, a woman that he'd longed for most of his adult life. And what a sweet kiss it had been, made all the sweeter because he'd waited *years* to kiss Jenna. And he wasn't disappointed.

Both kisses had rocked him to the soles of his feet and all the places in between. He'd wanted to wrap his arms around her and crush her body to his. He'd wanted to take her into his bed and make love to her.

He sighed. He'd just have to live with the

memory of Jenna's kisses, but that galled him. After tasting her sweetness, he wanted more.

Looking out the window to the backyard, he watched as she swam laps, the water sluicing over her shapely curves.

Jenna didn't need that silly magazine article. Nor did she need to be made up for a TV commercial ever again. Her natural beauty and personality were just fine. Perfect, in fact.

But obviously Jenna was trying to change herself for someone—someone who didn't appreciate her as she was. Just thinking about the ignorant fool who'd captured Jenna's attention made his blood boil.

What kind of an idiot was this guy?

Then it hit him. Could he dare hope that *he* was the one that Jenna was trying to seduce?

Nah.

But *could* he be the one?

If he was, he was one lucky cowboy—and there wasn't another with a thicker skull.

He watched as Jenna executed a perfect jackknife. Damn, he was hot and sweaty, and the cast was itchy. What he wouldn't give to join Jenna in the pool.

But maybe…

No.

Okay, so maybe Dustin did have a well-deserved reputation for being a ladies' man for a few years. And maybe that reputation had followed him into the present due to the inordinate amount of buckle bunnies who always hung around him.

Maybe he should have a talk with Tom and tell him that he'd like his permission—and blessing—to date his sister. But if Tom told him no, then what? Would he date Jenna anyway? Would that be the end of his friendship with Tom?

Or maybe he was completely mistaken that he was the object of Jenna's attention, and he was hoping against hope.

But just the idea that he *was* the one sure made a cowboy feel good, even if it did pose a whole new set of problems that he'd have to deal with sooner or later.

After leaving the pool and managing to avoid Dustin, Jenna changed quickly into a pair of white twill pants and a royal-blue tank top. She slid back into her flip-flops and grabbed her keys. She was going to pick up Andy at school and talk to his summer school teacher, Mrs. Cummings. She wanted to know if there had been an improvement in Andy's reading and math work.

Besides, she had to get away from Dustin for a while and think.

As she drove, she thought about how his bare, muscled chest had felt beneath her hands. She'd known he was in good shape, but she hadn't been prepared for the heat that coursed through her body at the touch of his warm skin.

Jenna found a parking space in the front row of the parking lot and hurried into the school. The buses were lined up, and she wanted to catch Andy before he boarded.

St. Margaret's Grammar School was the school she and Tom had attended from kindergarten through eighth grade. The sisters were strict, yet caring, and they taught more than just the three R's.

She headed for the office and wasn't surprised to find Sister Elizabeth John still there. Her eighth-grade teacher was now the principal.

Sister was surprised to see Jenna. "What brings you here? It's lovely to see you."

"I came to talk to Mrs. Cummings and to give my nephew, Andy, a ride home."

"Go right ahead. Fifth classroom on the left by the cafeteria."

"Got it."

Jenna peeked through the class door and saw Andy sitting in the front row. Mrs. Cummings was going through a decimal problem on the blackboard, and called on Andy to answer.

He sat up straighter, then grinned as he figured out the answer.

"If my dad rides his bull for 2.3 seconds, Uncle Dustin rides for 7.35 seconds, and Adriano rides for 4 seconds, the total seconds are 13.65. The average of the three rides is 4.55 seconds. A little over half of what they need for a full eight-second ride."

"Excellent, Andy! Excellent." Mrs. Cummings clapped. "Of course, the problem is not about bull rides, but your answer is correct. Bravo!"

Bravo to Dustin, too, Jenna thought. It was Dustin who had figured out how to make learning fun for Andy, whereas Jenna had just bored her nephew senseless.

She remembered Dustin hunched over, intent on helping Andy with his math. It was quite the picture—a big cowboy helping a little boy. What a sweet man.

"Aunt Jenna...hi!"

As the classroom emptied out, Andy's voice penetrated her daydreams.

"Hi, honey. I heard your answer to that problem, and I'm so proud of you!"

Andy grinned. It warmed Jenna's heart to watch kids regain their confidence after a setback.

Mrs. Cummings walked toward them. She shook her head, smiling. "There's great improvement in Andy's math skills."

"How's his reading coming along, Mrs. Cummings?"

She saw a moment of hesitation from the teacher. "Andy's much improved in his reading, but we're going to continue to work on it."

"I'll work on it more with him at home, too. Thanks for everything," Jenna said.

As they walked on the gleaming floor with light green lockers on both sides, Jenna turned to Andy. "I think this great report merits some ice cream. Don't you think, Andy?"

"Sure!"

Jenna drove to an ice cream stand. They both ordered chocolate cones with sprinkles and ate them in the car, talking and laughing. When she pulled into the driveway of the Bar R, she saw Andy scanning the area. She was almost positive that Andy was looking for Dustin, just as she was.

Jenna forced herself to concentrate on parking the car, but then Andy let out a hoot when he spotted him.

"There's Uncle Dustin sitting on the porch," Andy said.

Jenna had seen him, too, and her stomach did a little flutter. She remembered how his lips had felt on hers—warm and tender—and she wanted more.

When she turned the vehicle off, she heard the click of Andy's seat belt. He grabbed his backpack and ran in the direction of the porch.

She saw the two of them speak, then Andy pulled a book out of his backpack and handed it to Dustin.

Jenna could hazard a guess by the color of the book's cover that it was Andy's reading book.

Was Dustin going to try to make the next reading lesson fun for Andy?

She hoped so.

Jenna felt a tug of jealousy. Here she was a professional teacher, and a cowboy without any teaching credentials was able to help Andy more than she.

As long as Andy was learning, what did it matter?

It didn't, she resolved, walking up the porch steps.

"Gentlemen, dinner will be ready in an hour, give or take." She was going to make burgers.

"Sounds good," Dustin said. "Can I help?"

She didn't know if she could be with him in the small confines of the kitchen. Didn't know if she was ready to inhale his masculine scent, or feel his wary gaze on her.

"No, you stay here and hang out with Andy. I have everything under control."

If only she did…

Chapter Six

Dustin rifled through Andy's reading book, but his mind was on Jenna. She was completely unaware of how beautiful she was.

"There's good stories in your book, Andy," Dustin said.

"Nah."

"Really. They look interesting," Dustin stated.

"Humpf," was Andy's reply.

Dustin figured that Andy would come around if he didn't push too hard. Sure enough, Andy soon got curious, and by the time Jenna announced that dinner was ready, Andy had read a story about saguaro cactus aloud to Dustin. They had a lively discussion about it at dinner.

But all the while, Dustin's mind was really on Jenna and the kisses that they shared. It was difficult being natural when all he wanted to do was to kiss her again. He tried to concentrate on Andy, but his gaze drifted to Jenna's lips.

It seemed that Jenna was focused on teaching Andy, but on several occasions, she turned to him and nodded, flashing him a big smile.

Damn. It made him happy when she smiled, made his day brighter.

As far as Jenna was concerned, if Dustin could get Andy interested in reading about saguaro cactus, then he could do anything.

As they were finishing dinner and Andy was excused to go play basketball, Dustin leaned over the table. "While you were visiting Andy at school, I found a magazine by the pool that I think might be yours. I put it on the coffee table in the living room."

"Magazine?" Her stomach churned. "Oh, yes. Thanks. I never finished reading it." She waved at the air, as if dismissing the importance of the magazine.

"Uh, Jenna?" he asked.

"Yes?"

"You looked great today. You know, during the taping of the commercial."

That was nice of him to say. She stopped in mid-bite. "I felt a little...odd, getting all fussed over, but it was interesting and a lot of fun. I can't wait until the commercial comes out."

"It was fun." He paused, as if working up enough courage to continue.

She waited, her stomach in knots.

"And Jenna?"

"Yes?"

"About that kiss..."

Her mouth went dry. "Yes."

"It was just part of the commercial. It didn't mean anything," Dustin said, his blue eyes locked on hers.

She shrugged and shot him an expression that conveyed it meant even less to her. "Of course. It didn't mean a thing. It was just acting."

She got up and started washing the pots and pans in the sink, scrubbing them within an inch of their lives.

Didn't mean anything? Wasn't he the one who kissed her first, when it wasn't in the script? Wasn't he the one who ran his finger down her cheek? That wasn't in the script, either.

That wasn't an act. He'd wanted to kiss her.

Jenna stole a glance at Dustin, but he caught her.

"What's wrong?" he asked quickly.

"Um… I just thought of something I forgot to do," she lied.

She tried to think over her wildly pounding heart.

Could Dustin possibly be lying to her, too? And why would he do that?

After the meal she'd just made, Jenna decided that she could use a little exercise. She missed doing her yoga routine. She hadn't done it since she'd arrived at the Bar R.

Changing into a pair of black yoga pants and a black sports bra, she grabbed her yoga mat and went outside to find a place where she could exercise without being disturbed.

She noticed Dustin talking to Andy and a couple of the ranch hands on the front porch. Jenna wondered if there were any issues about the ranch that she needed to address, but it seemed that Dustin was handling things. Good.

She noticed Andy walked toward the bunk-

house with the ranch hands, bouncing a basketball, probably hoping for a pickup game.
Dustin settled into his favorite rocking chair
on the porch.

Jenna decided that doing yoga by the pool
would be the best place, so she cut through
the wooden door that led to the backyard.

Facing the setting sun, she began her exercises with long, languid stretches—and then
launched into several yoga positions.

She tried to concentrate on what she was
doing, but she kept rehashing the commercial shoot.

*Over by the lounge chair was where he
first saw her in the colorful bikini. Over by
the palm was where she first kissed Dustin.
On the second shot, they'd kissed again.*

She tried to clear her mind and concentrate
on her stretching and breathing, but Dustin—
the way he looked without his shirt on, the
way he'd kissed her with contained passion,
his smile, how he helped Andy—well, she
just couldn't keep him from intruding on her
thoughts.

She stood tall, starting the Salute to the
Sun series, but out of the corner of her eye,
she caught a flash of metal.

Crutches.

Dustin.

She turned to face him.

"I'm sorry," he said. "I didn't mean to disturb you. I just wanted to ask you something, but it can wait. Please continue." He walked over to a lounge chair and slid into it.

He didn't look sorry at all. Matter of fact, he was grinning.

But how could she continue with him watching her?

She couldn't.

Woman's Universe would advise her to take advantage of the situation, but that just wasn't...her.

Jenna rolled up her yoga mat and walked over to where Dustin was sitting.

"Believe it or not, I do some of those stretching exercises before every event. The PBR had a yoga instructor do a presentation with the thought that it might help us limber up, reduce injuries." He knocked on his cast. "Cowabunga had his mind set on running me over, so nothing could have helped me."

"You ran and dodged him as best you could, but he was like a freight train bearing down on you. And when he rolled you around on the dirt with his horns..." She shook her head, remembering how scared she'd been.

He raised an eyebrow. "It almost sounds like you care."

"Of course I care, Dustin," she snapped. Why couldn't he see that she'd always cared about him?

His eyebrows raised, just a little. "Well, thanks. And thanks for helping me out."

"What did you want to ask me?" she said.

"I'm so damn bored. I want to do something— anything."

"Like what?" she asked. "Like paint?"

"I wouldn't mind. It would keep me busy."

"I'd be happy to get your supplies from your apartment."

"Thanks, but—" He shrugged, then looked in the direction of the ranch hands.

"Are you afraid that they'll think you're not a real cowboy if you paint?"

"I just like being anonymous," he said quietly.

She shook her head. "Then paint in the kitchen. No one will know except Andy and me. Make me a list of what you'll need."

"Okay."

Jenna handed him a sheet of paper and a pen, and Dustin listed the supplies that he'd need, but his heart wasn't really in it. He could think of better things to do with Jenna than paint!

"Watch Andy for me. I'll be back in a while."

Dustin raised his eyebrows. "You're going *now?*"

"Sure."

Jenna felt his eyes on her as she headed into the house. She felt lighter, happier. This would give Dustin something to do, and she could watch him draw and paint. Fascinating.

A talent like his shouldn't be wasted, and she was going to do everything in her power to encourage him.

Dustin didn't want to paint. He wanted to hit the honky-tonks with Jenna.

He could picture her in his arms, moving to the music. Imagined kissing her again... imagined Tom breaking his other leg...

He looked down at his cast and swore under his breath just as Jenna came bounding out the front door and raced down the steps.

"Need anything else from your apartment?" she asked.

"I'm good. Just be careful driving."

"It almost seems as though you care," she said, echoing his prior words. Smiling, she got into her car and drove off.

I do care, Jenna. I've always cared.

He flipped open his cell and left another message for Tom. The sooner he talked to him, the better.

He'd told Jenna that their kisses didn't mean anything to him only because he couldn't let things go further until—unless—he got the green light from Tom. Because kissing her again would only lead to bed.

And that couldn't happen.

What a cozy scene, Jenna thought.

Andy was doing his homework at the kitchen table. Dustin was sketching on a big white pad and she was reading *Pride and Prejudice,* her favorite book, for about the hundredth time.

And she wondered, for about the two hundredth time, if Dustin was as clueless as Darcy.

I could get used to this, Jenna thought. If she closed her eyes, she could imagine a family of her own. The children studying, Dustin sketching or painting and she'd be reading.

Interesting how she'd put Dustin into her dream.

Soon, she noticed Andy's struggling to keep his eyes open.

"Andy, why don't you get ready for bed," she said.

He nodded. Standing slowly, he shook Dustin's hand and hugged Jenna around the neck. She patted his back.

Andy was old enough to take himself to bed, but she tagged along anyway.

"You like Uncle Dustin, don'cha?" Andy asked.

She nodded. "Sure. I like him," she said casually.

Andy tugged his T-shirt over his head. "He likes you."

"Oh, yeah?"

"Yeah. I see him looking at you."

She was about to pump the boy for more information, but restrained herself.

"Don't forget to brush your teeth, Andy," she instructed like a dutiful aunt.

She waited until Andy came back from the bathroom, then she tucked him into bed.

"I miss my mother," Andy said. "But I'm glad you're here, Aunt Jenna."

In all the time she'd been at the Bar R, Marla, Andy's mother, had never even called to talk to him.

"I know you miss her." Jenna hugged him and planted a noisy kiss on the boy's forehead that made him laugh. "I love you, Andy. Always remember that."

"I—I y-you…" There was no more forthcoming, Andy was sleeping.

She longed to give Marla a piece of her mind. How dare she ignore her son? Jenna just couldn't understand it. Her temper flared, but she tamped it back. She tucked the bed linens around Andy, gently kissed him on the forehead, then returned to the kitchen. She hurried over to the phone that was hanging on the wall, flipping through Tom's phone book.

"Everything okay?" Dustin asked.

"I'm just calling Marla. How dare she ignore her son!"

Marla didn't answer. Instead, a woman who identified herself as the housekeeper said that Miss Marla was in Cancún "with Mr. Josh."

"When are they expected back?"

"Two weeks."

"Do you have a number where they can be reached?"

The woman giggled. "They are on their honeymoon, but I have a number somewhere…"

"Never mind," Jenna said, hanging up the phone.

She leaned back against the wall, letting this new information sink in, wondering if Andy even knew that his mother had married again.

Jenna sighed. "I feel bad. He misses his mother."

"I overheard you on the phone. Marla's on her honeymoon?"

"With someone named Josh."

"Josh Eliott," Dustin replied. "I saw them together a couple of times at the Houston Livestock Show and Rodeo. He's a steer wrestler."

"Does Tom know?"

"Probably."

"I don't think he told Andy about Marla."

"Probably not. The last I knew he was waiting for a good time."

"I think the time is now," Jenna said. How could her brother not be around at a time like this? Or was Tom running away himself? She wondered if Tom still had feelings for Marla. Well, it was none of her business, but she'd make it her business if it concerned Andy.

She sat down at the table, but didn't pick up her book. Instead, she tapped her fingers on the table.

"I heard you with Andy on several occasions. You'd make a good mother," Dustin said.

She raised an eyebrow. "You think so?"

"I do."

"I think you'd make a good father. You're wonderful with Andy, too. You've helped him learn a lot."

"I'd love to be a father," he said quietly, then met Jenna's eyes. "Andy's going to pass to fifth grade."

She nodded. "We just have to make reading fun for him. Can you think of any books or magazines that would keep his interest?"

"The *Pro Bull Rider* magazine," Dustin said. "I have a copy in my duffel. It'd be perfect."

"Thanks, Dustin," she replied, then paused. "How many?"

He raised an eyebrow. "How many what?"

"How many kids would you like to have?"

He laughed. "Forty-five."

"I didn't ask you how many of the top bull riders would ride in Vegas." She chuckled.

"I'd like as many as I was blessed with." He looked deep into her eyes, and she felt her cheeks burn.

The thought of having children with Dustin made her feel warm all over. That's what she'd wanted before—children of her own—but since her "turning thirty" midlife crisis she'd mapped out a different course for her way-too-dull life.

"And, of course, I want a ranch," Dustin continued. "That's what I'm working for, Jenna. My own spread. I want to win the World Finals and retire."

"Good for you," she said. "That's a great goal."

"And what about you?"

"I want to travel, see the world, have adventures. I might teach in China for a year."

Dustin looked as if he'd just got head-butted by a raging bull.

"China? For a year? I didn't think that— I mean I thought that we'd—"

"We'd *what?*" she asked.

"Nothing. My mistake." He looked down at his hands that were intertwined together as if in prayer.

Jenna suddenly felt confused, weary. Dustin's plan of a home and children was appealing to her, but that was her old dream. Wasn't it? Besides, his plan didn't include *her*. She didn't know if it ever would.

"I'm tired," she said, sadness suddenly welling in her chest. She pushed herself from the chair, noticing the disappointment on Dustin's face.

Was it because she was leaving or was it something she'd said?

Chapter Seven

Dustin scratched his head.

They were having a good conversation. Why the sudden departure?

Dustin struggled to his feet and reached for his crutches. He was going to knock on her bedroom door and finish the conversation they'd started.

When Jenna answered the door, she greeted him with a thin smile, her green eyes misty.

Had she been crying?

He moved toward her, then stopped. What had he come here for?

Cursing under his breath, he pulled her toward him. His mouth slanted over hers, gentle at first, then demanding.

Then he broke away, raising his eyes to the sky.

"What am I doing?" he asked.

Jenna smiled. He took it as a sign that she wanted him to continue.

"We're making out." She chuckled.

"This isn't high school."

"No, it's not. It's better. Now, kiss me again, Dustin Morgan."

He did. He kissed her with every ounce of built-up passion that he'd had since high school.

"I want to take you to bed," he said.

This is it! Thank you Woman's Universe!

Dustin kissed her hand, and instead of being happy, a fog of sadness settled over her. Lately, she just wasn't herself—the big hair, the flirting, the bikini—all that was someone else.

Yet, Dustin wanted to kiss that someone else. He wanted to take that person to bed, not the real Jenna Reed.

What had she done?

She'd lost her mind.

"Jenna?" Dustin rubbed her back. "Did you hear what I said?"

"Yes. I—I did." She'd just wanted a fling, and now it seemed like the person who was about to have the fling wasn't even her.

"And?"

"Dustin, I just can't. It's not me you want." Regret welled in her chest. She walked to the bedroom door and motioned for him to leave. It was one of the hardest things she'd ever done in her life. "You'd better leave."

"Whatever you say." Dustin looked like she'd landed a sucker punch to his gut. In a way, she had.

"I'm so…sorry, Dustin. I'm really sorry."

It's not me you want.

What on earth did that mean?

Was she talking about that lame magazine article? He didn't fall for that stuff.

Oh, who was he kidding? He did fall for it. He fell for it all. And he wanted to think that Jenna had gone to all that trouble just for him, but he didn't know for sure.

She needn't have. Jenna was special just the way she was.

He didn't move. He just stood there like a lump—a broken-down lump of a bull rider who was still mooning over his best friend's very off-limits sister.

Even if he somehow conveniently forgot about his promise to Tom, how was he supposed to make love to Jenna with half his leg in a cast? Well, there were ways, but their first time together should be everything that he'd been dreaming of for all these many years.

He wondered if she was a virgin. Judging by her reliance on a magazine article, she wasn't all that experienced.

He should just come out and ask her if he was the one who she'd been trying to seduce.

There wasn't a bull he was scared to ride, but he was too chicken to hear Jenna's answer.

Later that night, Jenna sat in her room mulling over the past few days, and her experiments in the art of seduction.

Somewhere between the big hair and the makeup, she'd lost herself.

Yet in spite of everything, the Ten Ways had worked! She should be thrilled. Dustin wanted to take her to bed. Wasn't that what she wanted?

After a restless night, Jenna got up early and made coffee. Sitting on a rocker on the front porch, she sipped the strong brew, still thinking of the events of the day before.

With any luck, Dustin wouldn't mention any of it.

The door sprang open, and Dustin hobbled out. "I smelled coffee."

Jenna got to her feet, searching his face and eyes for amusement, but there was none. "I'll get you a cup. Sit." She held the chair still for him. "You take it black, right?"

"Thanks," he said.

She roused Andy from his bed and instructed the sleepy boy to wash his face, comb his hair and get ready for school. Then she went into the kitchen to get Dustin a cup of coffee.

Back on the porch, she handed the coffee to Dustin. "It's so strong that a horseshoe could float on it."

"Perfect," he said.

"Dustin, about yesterday…and before… when I—I was trying to…"

He held up a hand to stop her. "Don't worry about it. I didn't mean what I said."

She raised an eyebrow. "About what?"

He looked at the door, then lowered his voice. "About us. About us sleeping together. It's a bad idea. I shouldn't have brought it up."

"Oh," she said, trying to swallow the lump in her throat. "I see."

"And I hope that the guy you like knows that he's one lucky stiff."

"I don't think he does."

Dustin grunted. "Then he's a fool."

Jenna bit back a smile. "No doubt about that."

Feeling restless, Jenna decided to go for a ride. So she saddled up a palomino by the name of Sparky. She always rode Sparky when visiting Tom and thought of the horse as her own.

Just as she was ready to mount, she felt someone watching her. Looking up, she saw Dustin silhouetted in the barn door.

"Hi," he said. "Wish I could join you. I'd love to go for a ride."

She shook her head. "Sorry."

He tapped the cast with the point of a crutch. "Just four more weeks with this thing," he said.

She felt an ache around her heart. He'd be leaving soon. Actually, so would she. Summer school ended in about three weeks, and Tom would be home.

She wouldn't be needed anymore.

Suddenly, she felt lonely.

But she'd be going back to school and she'd have a whole bunch of new kids to get to know. They'd keep her busy and keep her mind off Dustin.

"Need help?" he asked.

She laughed. "Did you forget that I was born on a ranch?"

"Not at all."

There was a long pause. Then he pushed his hat back.

"Damn. I forgot to tell you." He held up his cell phone. "Tom just called. He thought he'd catch Andy, but he missed him. He said he won the Memphis and the Billings events."

"Great!"

"He's leading the standings now," Dustin said.

"And now you're second."

"I expected that. I expect to be even lower as more time goes by. But the PBR's summer break will be coming up soon, so things will be at a standstill."

She took Sparky's reins and led her out of the barn. Dustin followed, then rubbed the horse's nose as she mounted.

"Where are you riding?" he asked.

"The ATV trails through the saguaros, then

through the meadow. Just an easy ride; it's been a long time for me."

"Have a good time," he said, moving away from the horse.

Jenna walked Sparky behind the bunk-house toward the start of the trail, and won-dered if perhaps Dustin had wanted to talk to her.

She wondered what was on his mind.

He probably just wanted to reiterate that he didn't want to take her to bed.

Message already received.

She tried to erase the cardboard Jenna—the Jenna of the commercial and the Ten Ways—from her mind. She was going to go back to her regular self. She was a book freak, a sub-urban teacher, a mentor of two of her school district's most academic clubs, a rancher's daughter, a sister and an aunt.

She'd never give up her quest for adven-ture and love. But maybe she'd just go back to being herself and see what happened.

It was probably stupid of him to ride the ATV with his ankle in a cast, but he found that he could operate the hand controls quite easily.

With his crutches bungeed to the back, he

took off down the path, following Jenna. He drove slowly so he wouldn't scare the palomino.

He paused at the trail where it opened up to the meadow, a kind of misnomer here in the desert. It was just a field with low scruffy vegetation. He and Tom rode ATVs and horses here all the time, but now Jenna was enjoying it.

As she trotted Sparky, her hair blew back in the breeze, its golden color shining even lighter in the afternoon sun.

Dustin could watch her all day. Her jeans were taut across her butt, and she wore a royal blue T-shirt and cowboy boots.

He liked this Jenna. He felt comfortable with her.

When he turned the handle with a little too much power, the ATV lunged forward. Jenna or Sparky must have heard it. Distracted, she turned sharply. Her horse stopped abruptly, and she fell from the saddle.

Dustin cranked up the ATV and hurried to where she'd fallen. He slid from the machine and hit the ground next to her.

"Are you okay?" he asked. "I'm sorry, Jenna. I didn't mean to scare you." His ankle throbbed, but he shook the feeling off. Instead, he pushed his body up with his hands to check her for injuries.

She stared up at him, her face flushed.

"Jenna, talk to me."

"You idiot," she yelled. "Don't you know better than to scare a horse?"

"I do know better."

She lifted up her head, and he slipped his hand under it as a cushion.

"I gave it too much juice. It just roared. I'm sorry."

She began to laugh. "I'm okay. Are you?"

He glanced down at the desert dirt all over his cast, hands and clothes.

"I'll live."

Dustin didn't make a move to get up. All he could think of was getting another taste of Jenna. He stared at her lips, and her smile faded. He looked into her eyes and twin emeralds looked back at him, a touch darker than usual.

He bent his head to kiss her and felt her hand around his neck, holding him close. With a slight groan, she met him halfway.

He tried to move, tried to feel the length of her body against his. It was impossible to position himself, but Jenna managed. Without taking her lips from his, she slipped under him. He felt her hands on his cheeks, down his neck, down the front of his shirt. He inhaled the sweetness of her, the smell of the sunshine on her clothes.

He moved as if in a dream, a dream that Jenna had starred in for so many years.

That reminded him of his promise to Tom. *Tom.*

He'd forgotten to tell her that Tom wanted her to call him. That's why he'd followed her, he told himself. It was because of Tom.

He moved away, smiling down at her. She raised an eyebrow as if to question why he'd broken the kiss. "I forgot to tell you that your brother wants you to call him."

She remained silent.

"It's nothing important. He just wants to talk to you about Andy's progress," Dustin explained.

"Okay," she said, scrambling to get up and dusting off her clothes. She didn't look at him.

Sparky was grazing nearby. Jenna gave a whistle, and the horse came walking to her.

He wished he could get up and not lie in the dirt like a snake, but his crutches were bungeed to the back of the ATV.

"Jenna, my crutches are..."

"On the ATV." Brushing off her clothes as

she walked to the vehicle, she unhooked his crutches. Then she held them in place as he gripped them to boost himself up.

"Hold them tight."

"Dustin, I know the drill by now."

"Sorry," he said sheepishly.

With several grunts, he was able to stand up. She handed him the crutches and he slid them under his arms. Then he doubled over in pain.

"Dustin! Are you okay?"

"I'm all right. I just landed at the wrong angle."

"Maybe I should take you to the emergency room. Or at least to your doctor."

"I'll be okay."

"Don't be so damn stubborn!"

"Thanks, Jenna, but I'll be fine. I'll take it easy for a while." Sweat broke out on his forehead and upper lip. His ankle had bothered him before, but instead of changing its position, he'd kept kissing her. "It seems like I'm always thanking you."

"We've made progress, at least," she said. "Before, you wanted to do everything yourself. Remember?"

His eyes dropped to her lips. "There's some things that you just can't do yourself."

She smiled, knowing exactly what he meant, then climbed back on Sparky.

"I'll be back in a while," she said, then smiled even wider. "Then I'll make that important call to Tom, the one that you came all the way out here to tell me about."

She knew.

She knew that the forgotten phone call wasn't the only thing that had gotten him out here. He'd wanted to be with her.

The kisses were a bonus.

When he got back to the house, he hobbled up the porch, then collapsed into his usual rocking chair. He dialed Tom's number.

"Hello?"

"Hey, partner. I have a question for you. Remember way back in high school, freshman year, you made me promise to stay away from Jenna?"

"Yeah. I remember it clearly. Why?"

"I was just wondering if you're going to hold me to that promise." Dustin found himself holding his breath.

Tom was silent for a moment. "What the hell's been going on between you and my sister?"

"Nothing. Nothing. Just answer the question," Dustin said impatiently.

"Don't touch her, Dustin. This is my sister we're talking about. She's not one of your buckle bunnies."

"When was the last time you've seen me with a buckle bunny, Tom? Tell me."

Silence. "It's just that…well, Jenna's my sister. I don't want her to be another notch on your belt."

"Jenna's a grown woman with a mind of her own."

"I'm still holding you to that promise, cowboy. Jenna's something special."

"Damn it. I know that."

Tom clicked off the phone, and Dustin gritted his teeth until his jaw hurt.

What should he do now?

Should he go against his best friend's wishes and finally go after the girl of his dreams?

Jenna slowly paged through Dustin's sketch pad, not able to put it down. It wasn't as if she was invading his privacy, she told herself. She was just admiring his talent.

If he ever decided to stop riding bulls, there would certainly be a market for his paintings. His well-known name and legion of fans certainly wouldn't hurt, either.

He was also talented in other areas—the cowboy sure could kiss.

But why had he broken off their kisses so suddenly?

She knew his ankle was bothering him. She could understand that. He shouldn't have slid off the ATV to come to her assistance.

One thing she was sure of—now that she'd dumped the magazine and was back to herself, she didn't want to wait another sixteen years for Dustin to make another move.

The kitchen phone rang, and she picked it up.

"Hey."

"Tom! I was just about to call you. I hear you're winning event after event."

"I'm doing good. How's Andy doing?"

"Fabulous. I spoke with his teacher, and he's making progress. We have to work on his reading a little more."

"I can't thank you enough, Jenna."

"You'd better thank Dustin, too. He had a lot to do with teaching Andy."

"He did?"

"Absolutely."

There was silence, and Jenna wondered why. Her brother was never at a loss for words.

"Tom?"

"How is everything else going?"

"Everything's fine. Your ranch is running smoothly."

"Um… What about Dustin?"

Her cheeks heated. "What about him?"

"Everything okay?"

I want him, but he doesn't seem to want me.

She flushed if her brother could read her mind. "Oh, he's just impatient to get his cast off."

"Anything else I ought to know…uh… about Dustin?"

What was Tom fishing for?

"Not a thing."

"And you? Are you okay?"

"Tom, what are you trying *not* to ask?"

"Can't a brother just ask if you're okay?"

"I'm fine. We're all fine. If you're trying to ask me if you can stay on the road longer and hit more events, it's okay with me. Andy misses you, but I think he understands."

"Jenna, I'll be in Wickenburg for a bull riding on Saturday night. Do you think that Andy might want to attend? And Dustin, of course. Bring Dustin. I need to talk to him, get caught up."

"I'm sure they'd love to go."

"Great!" Tom said. "I'll call Andy about it later. And call me if you need me."

"I will."

"And Jenna?"

"Yeah?"

"Take care of yourself."

"I always do."

Jenna hung up the phone. Her brother was acting a bit strange. But for sure Andy would love to see his father and watch him ride, and Dustin was bored out of his mind.

Wickenburg was a little over three hours away, an easy drive, mostly on Interstate 10 West. Going to a bull-riding event was a win-win all the way around.

An extra bonus would be the fact that she'd be able to spend the day with Dustin.

Chapter Eight

Jenna drove the ranch's big red pickup down I-10 West.

Andy was so excited that he was ready to jump out of his jeans and boots. He'd been talking bull-riding stats nonstop, and about all the bull riders he would see. It would be the icing on the cake if his father won the event.

Dustin was mostly quiet, answering Andy with even more stats and riding percentages of the bulls.

Jenna had printed off the draw sheet and was aghast that Tom had drawn Dustin's nemesis, Cowabunga, in the long-go round.

"I hope my dad rides Cowabunga. He'll show that bull," Andy said.

"He sure will, partner. He sure will," Dustin said.

Even though Dustin carried on a lively conversation with Andy, he answered Jenna in short, terse sentences. It was as if he'd rather be anywhere else than in a tight truck cab with her.

Jenna pulled into a rest area for a bathroom break and for Dustin to stretch as much as he could. At the rest stop, Native Americans were selling jewelry and baskets, and Jenna paused to admire a green turquoise necklace that had caught her eye.

Soon Dustin was peeling off bills and handing them to the woman.

"What are you doing?" Jenna asked.

"I'm buying you a necklace," he said, waving off his change, and motioning to Jenna. "Turn around."

A rush of heat settled on her cheeks. "Dustin, you don't have to buy me—"

"It's my pleasure."

"But—"

"Jenna, it's nothing," he said tersely. "Turn around."

Tears pricked at her eyes. It had meant

something to her. Dutifully, she turned around and lifted her hair up.

She heard him mumble, "This darn thing."

She turned and took it from his hands, unfastening the clasp for him. Handing it back, his hand closed around hers and lingered. Turning around, she tried to catch her breath.

She felt his knuckles skim the back of her neck.

"Lift your hair up again," he whispered, and she could feel the warmth of his breath.

The cool stones rested against her skin as he fumbled trying to fasten the necklace.

"Got it," he said.

She turned toward him. "What do you think?"

He gazed into her eyes. "Beautiful."

Her heart pounded wildly because he wasn't even looking at the necklace. He was looking at her.

Time didn't move. They didn't move. Until finally Dustin's eyes dropped to the green-blue stones.

He cleared his throat. "Beautiful," he said again, then turned and went to the truck, leaving her standing there. Suddenly, he stopped, and she waited for him to turn back. She wondered, hoped that he'd say something, anything.

But he didn't. He shook his head, then continued on.

"Thank you, Dustin," she whispered, fingering the necklace.

It didn't matter if it didn't mean anything to him—it meant everything to her.

Dustin longed to tell Jenna how he felt about her.

But he couldn't. Tom still stood between them.

It was getting harder and harder to keep his promise, though. So maybe it was time to move back to his apartment in Tubac.

But how could he leave Jenna?

In spite of his injury, this summer had been the best time of his life. He didn't want to cut his time short. After more than sixteen years of longing for Jenna, didn't he owe it to himself?

He swore under his breath. He was tired of psychoanalyzing everything from a dozen different angles.

He'd promised Tom that he'd oversee his ranch. But he'd also promised Tom that he'd stay away from Jenna.

Jenna walked toward the car with Andy, her blond hair shimmering in the sunlight. If it wasn't for Andy's chatter, there would have been complete silence on the rest of the ride, but the boy didn't seem to notice.

"There's a fair going on!" Andy explained as they caught sight of the rodeo grounds.

Dustin checked his watch. They had time to grab a bite to eat, let Andy hit some rides and visit Tom behind the chutes.

Dustin wasn't particularly looking forward to meeting up with Tom. He hoped that he and his friend could remain civil to one another.

"How about some barbecue?" Dustin asked, pointing with his crutch to a stand.

"Sounds great," Jenna said. "How about it, Andy?"

"Can I just have a cheeseburger?"

Dustin laid a hand on the little boy's shoulder. "Sure. They have those, too. And nachos with cheese sauce."

"Awesome."

They sat at a picnic table under the shade of a tent complete with ceiling fans.

"Will you go on some rides with me, Aunt Jenna?"

"How about the merry-go-round?" she asked, then chuckled.

"That's for sissies," Andy replied.

Jenna shrugged and made a sad face. "Then I'll have to go alone."

"I'll go with you," Dustin said quickly, shocking himself with the intensity of his statement. Jenna even looked at him strangely.

"I mean, that's about the biggest ride I can handle with this cast," he said, trying to look less eager.

They waited as Andy rode on every ride that plunged, pivoted and did a free fall to earth. While they were waiting, he noticed that Jenna sometimes touched the necklace he'd given her or fingered the silver chain. She seemed to be thinking.

He hoped that she was thinking about how pleased she was with the necklace.

Andy ran into a friend, Kyle, from school, and the boys went off with Kyle's parents to ride the roller coaster for the fifth time.

"How about that ride on the merry-go-round, Jenna?"

She looked at him and shook her head. "I'm sure you're just dying to go."

"I'm game," he said.

He handed the attendant two tickets and hopped up on the platform.

"I like the pink one with the flowing black mane," she said, mounting the intricately carved wooden horse.

Dustin mounted the horse next to her—a lime-green one with a light blue mane—with his good leg.

Please don't let any of the guys see me.

Thankfully, no one did...with the exception of the biggest mouth in the Professional Bull Riders, Cord Fetters.

"Well, Dustin Morgan," Fetters said, stopping at the fence that ran around the ride. "Be careful you don't fall off."

Fetters would have it all over the arena within five minutes that he was riding a green-and-blue horse on the merry-go-ground.

Dustin closed his eyes. The flack from the guys was going to be hell, but it would be worth it to see Jenna enjoying herself.

"Fetters, would it do me any good to ask you to keep your mouth shut about this?" Dustin asked.

"Not a chance. This is good stuff. This is what legends are made of."

Fetters scurried off as the organ music began.

"I'm sorry, Dustin," Jenna said. "I didn't mean to make you a laughingstock of the PBR."

"Don't give it another thought."

"But you're never going to live this down."

"Yes, I will," he said quietly. "I've lived down other things that were more serious."

"But—"

"Shush." He put a finger over her lips. "Don't worry about me, Jenna. I'm doing exactly what I want to do, and this is where I want to be—with you."

He could swear that her eyes looked moist.

What was he doing? He had to stop telling her what was on his mind and what was in his heart.

He was only leading her on, and he wasn't that much of a cad.

So from now on, he needed to keep his mouth and heart lassoed tightly and not let those lovesick comments escape.

That'd be about as easy as riding a short-go bull for a full minute.

Dustin stood close behind Jenna as she pitched plastic rings around milk bottles at one of the game stands.

She could feel the warmth of his every breath on her cheek, the low timbre of his voice hypnotizing her.

He gripped her wrist and moved it back and forth. "Aim for one on the end. Not in the middle. Take it nice and slow, nice and slow."

She missed. The ring bounced off the bottle and hit the floor.

"Three more tries," said the game worker.

"How many rings do I need to get to win that stuffed tiger?" Jenna asked.

"Two," he said.

"You can do it, Jenna. Easy now. Let it go when you're ready."

"I'm ready, Dustin." That little phrase had more than one meaning for her. She really didn't care about the orange-and-black tiger, she just enjoyed being this close to him.

Dustin continued to murmur encouraging words. She let the ring fly and got the bottle. Then another.

She clapped her hands and turned to Dustin. He hugged her to him, then quickly released her as if she carried the plague.

Taking her prize, she studied it. It was just a cheap carnival prize, but it would always remind her of today.

"I think you need some cotton candy," Dustin said, moving slowly on his crutches. "I see a stand straight ahead."

"I haven't had cotton candy in years." Jenna's mouth was already watering.

"Well, it's a mandatory item at a country fair, so let's go."

She picked out pink, and as Dustin was paying, she looked at the Ferris wheel. And suddenly, she had the urge to go on the ride with him.

"Ride the Ferris wheel with me, Dustin," she blurted.

"Sure." He pushed his hat back with his thumb. "Let's do it."

The wait in line was brief, and he gave his crutches to the ticket taker to hold. Hopping on one foot to the ride, he flopped into the seat. Steadying it, Jenna slipped in next to him and locked the safety bar in place.

She was going to ride on a Ferris wheel with Dustin.

Would he kiss her?

She rolled her eyes. She was acting like a high school girl!

She plucked at her cotton candy as the ride jerked them back to allow other passengers to board.

They went around, stopping and going, until finally they made complete circles. Then the Ferris wheel paused about three-quarters around.

Dustin leaned over and pointed to the corner of her lips. "You have cotton candy there."

"Would you hold this?" she asked, handing him what was left of the spun sugar so she could look for a tissue in her purse.

Instead of taking it from her, he stared at her, his blue eyes not blinking.

"Dustin?"

He wrapped his arm around her shoulder, pulling her closer to him, closer still.

Studying her face, he seemed to be thinking. Funny, she'd always thought Dustin was a man of action.

She waited, wondered. Should she make a move?

But she didn't have to wait long as his warm, full lips touched hers. His tongue teased the corner of her lip, and she opened her mouth for him.

Their tongues warred as he crushed her to him, breathing heavily, his lips never leaving hers.

Just as abruptly he let her go and stared down at the ground.

This was becoming a habit with him. "Dustin, what happened? What's wrong?"

But he didn't answer. He continued to stare at the ground. Then he swore under his breath.

She followed his gaze to the midway, where Tom stood, watching them.

She waved to her brother, but for some reason, Tom didn't wave back.

When they got off the ride, Tom hugged Jenna close, glaring at Dustin behind her back.

Dustin held out his hand and they shook, but Tom's grip was stronger than usual.

"Where's Andy?" Tom asked.

"With a friend of his," Jenna explained. "We're meeting him in the Agriculture Building by the butter sculpture at six. That'll allow a lot of time for you to take him behind the chutes so he can talk to the riders and look at the bulls."

"Here's three tickets, front row, center," Tom handed Jenna the tickets, then turned to Dustin, "Would you mind bringing Andy behind the chutes? Jenna, you could hold the seats."

Dustin wondered why she'd have to hold the seats since they had tickets. He could tell by Jenna's furrowed brow that she was thinking the same thing. Then he realized that Tom didn't want Jenna around when they talked.

"Uh…okay," Jenna said.

Dustin was dreading the moment that they'd have a confrontation. Today might mark the demise of their friendship and the end of their partnership, because he planned to tell Tom what he felt for Jenna. If that wasn't good enough for him, then so be it.

But they never had a chance to talk. Riders surrounded Dustin most of the time, making small talk and asking when he was going to return to competition.

"A couple more months, then beware," Dustin said. "I'm going to shake up the standings."

Andy was grinning from ear to ear, and he hadn't left Tom's side. Of course, he'd missed his father, and it was obvious that Tom had missed Andy.

From his position, Dustin could see Jenna sitting in the arena. She was studying the draw sheet, and suddenly she looked up and met his gaze. She waved, and he waved back.

A heartbeat later, Tom and Andy stood next to him.

"I'll see you after the bull riding, slugger," Tom said to Andy.

"Okay, Dad."

"Then I'm off to Idaho. I'll be back home in about a week and can stay for a while."

"Ride 'em all, Dad, especially that Cow-abunga."

"You got it," Tom said. With a curt nod, he turned to Dustin.

"Andy, would you mind getting my bull rope over there?" he pointed to a lineup of ropes tied to a fence. "I want to show your Uncle Dustin something."

"Sure." Andy scurried off.

"I'm going to make this short and clear: stay away from Jenna. She's too good for you."

"I know that," Dustin whispered. "But I like her, Tom. I've *always* liked her. Always."

"You like every woman you've ever met," Tom said, meeting his gaze. "Look, Jenna isn't like the others you've been with."

"I know that."

"Jenna isn't…experienced. She hasn't dated much, and, well, let's face it, partner, you've been around. You have a reputation."

"I might have played the field, but with other women…well, it's just different. Jenna's special and I wouldn't do anything to hurt her. You have to believe me. I wouldn't lie to you."

"Okay. I guess you're right." Tom pushed his hat back and thought for a moment. "I still see Jenna as my little sister."

"She's not little anymore, dude. And you don't need to act as her father."

"I know, but…hey…" Andy appeared with Tom's bull rope, and that marked the end of their discussion. "Thanks, son," he said taking the rope from Andy. Then Tom turned to Dustin and nodded. "We'll talk more."

"I'm counting on that." Dustin tweaked his hat to his friend, and hoped that he would come around. Didn't Dustin deserve a chance at happiness? And he'd like to think that he could make Jenna happy, too. "Good luck tonight, partner. Call me."

Tom came in first in the long-go, and he rode Cowabunga for eight seconds without problems. He came in second in the overall standings.

After the event, there was a Team PBR autographing for the bull riders, and a line had already formed opposite Tom's place at one of the tables. There was no chance to continue the conversation with his friend.

Andy sat on a chair next to his father for a while, then began to tire.

"Time to hit the road," Jenna declared, motioning for Andy to join them.

After a traffic jam in the parking lot, they were back on I-10 heading to Tucson. It didn't take long for Andy to fall asleep between them. Right now, he was slumped on Dustin's left arm, and Dustin moved slowly to give the boy a more comfortable position.

"I had a wonderful time today," Jenna said, breaking the comfortable silence between them.

"Me, too."

He'd even ride the lime-green horse again if she asked.

He remembered their kiss on the Ferris wheel. Jenna tasted of candy and sugar, of carefree summer days and breezy summer nights.

They drove another five miles in silence until he spotted fireworks in the sky above one of the casinos off the interstate.

"I love fireworks," she said.

"Well, if you want to see them, get off at this exit," he said.

Clicking on her right turn signal to get off the highway, she came across a side street, where she pulled over to the side of the road where several other cars had stopped.

"Let's watch them from the tailgate," Jenna said getting out of the car. "But let's not wake Andy up. He's pooped."

Dustin hopped to the tailgate and released the latch, pulling it down. They both sat on it.

But he barely noticed the colorful explosions in the sky; he only had eyes for Jenna. How her nose was perfect in silhouette. How her lips were made for kissing. How beautiful she looked in the moonlight.

Dustin took her hand, and he was rewarded with a smile. She squeezed his.

"This is so…awesome," she said, using one of Andy's favorite words.

"You're awesome," Dustin replied.

He put his arm around Jenna and pulled her closer to him. She was just too far away.

Jenna leaned back on her hands and looked up into the sky, brilliant with fireworks and smiled. He could watch her all day.

"This is just a magical night, Dustin. I haven't been out like this in…" She lowered her voice. "Well, I'm embarrassed to say."

"Don't be embarrassed, Jenna, not with me."

"I am."

He rubbed his forehead. "What about?"

"Well, I know you read that magazine article. I left it open by the pool by mistake."

"Yeah, you did."

He'd like to lie to her, tell her that he hadn't read it, but he couldn't do that. He smiled slightly.

"Tell me, Jenna. Who's the man? Who were you trying to seduce?"

She rolled her eyes. "You don't know?"

"No."

Jenna hesitated. "It was all for you, Dustin."

"I thought so. I'd hoped, but—" He tweaked the brim of his hat. "Why thank you, ma'am," he said, exaggerating a drawl.

She laughed. "I am so embarrassed."

"Don't be. It's the best thing anyone's ever done for me."

As the fireworks exploded overhead, Dustin kissed the woman of his dreams.

Then he made a decision.

Tom might never come around. He took his position as head of the family too seriously. Besides, it hurt him down to his bones that his friend really didn't think he was good enough for Jenna.

But he wasn't going to think of the past, not tonight.

Tonight would be the culmination of a perfect day.

Chapter Nine

Jenna helped a sleepy Andy find his bed. He collapsed into it, clothes and all. She unlaced his sneakers and covered him with a blanket, giving him a kiss on the forehead.

Closing the boy's bedroom door, she went to the living room and noticed Dustin standing by the front door propped up by his crutches. He'd barely entered the house.

"Come with me, Jenna," he said softly, holding out his hand.

She knew what he wanted, where this was leading. She found herself holding her breath as she took his hand.

Turning her hand, he kissed the back of it, and she melted.

"I want you," he said. "I've wanted you for a very long time."

His words washed over her like a velvet fog. She wanted to tell him that she'd wanted him since…forever. But the words wouldn't come.

"I wish I could carry you to my bed," he said, and her knees almost buckled.

Jenna laid her palm on the side of his face and smiled. "Follow me."

The walk to his bedroom had never seemed so long. When she saw the queen bed in the guest room, she chuckled.

This wasn't the place of her dreams. Whenever she thought of making love with Dustin, she thought of lush green meadows and misty waterfalls—not Tom's guest room.

But she wouldn't change a thing.

"Undress for me, Jenna."

With shaky fingers, she fumbled with the buttons of her blouse. Finally, the garment was free and she tossed it on a chair. This moment with Dustin was what she'd been saving herself for, for more years than she'd care to remember. She'd never wanted another man.

Dustin nodded for her to continue. She

undid the clasp of her bra, and tossed it on top of her blouse. She stood in front of him, her breasts aching for his touch.

But he didn't touch her yet. "You're beautiful," he said, as heat rushed to her face.

"Your turn," she said, reaching for his shirt.

As she popped the snaps, her eyes never left his. When his shirt fell open, she ran her hands over the hard planes of his chest.

"You're beautiful, too," she said, then smiled.

He propped his crutches against the wall and shrugged out of his shirt, letting it fall to the ground. She helped him step out of his sweatpants and underwear.

Her eyes scanned his body. He was hard and strong, all of him.

"Kiss me, Dustin," she said softly.

"My pleasure."

As his lips slanted over hers, he crushed her to him, and she could see the evidence that he wanted her.

A tingling started low in her stomach, then gained intensity as it rippled out. This was Dustin Morgan, the man she'd fantasized about for years.

Dustin got comfortable on the bed, and she stretched out next to him. They lay together, kissing, smiling, touching and just happy to be in each other's company.

"Condom. My wallet," Dustin said, scanning the room. "Damn. It's in my pants."

"I'll get them," Jenna said, getting up. She picked up his pants from the floor and handed them to Dustin. Opening the wallet, he pulled out a foil packet.

In record time, he unrolled it over himself, and Jenna thought it was the sexiest thing she'd ever seen.

Her breathing came in short, deep pants, especially when Dustin pulled her on top of him.

She straddled him and, leaning over, kissed him as she guided him into her slowly. He filled her completely. She waited, not moving, just enjoying the sensations washing over her, wave after wave.

His hands were on her breasts, his fingers teasing her nipples, touching the green turquoise necklace that he'd said matched her eyes. It was the only thing that she hadn't taken off.

Her nipples were already hard, and now they ached. She wanted more. She began to move, feeling herself pulse around his hardness.

"Dustin," she moaned.

"I know," he said, breathlessly.

More waves washed over her, a forceful rush of physical and emotional release.

Then Dustin followed her over the edge.

Jenna had never experienced anything like this before. Granted, her experience was limited, but being with Dustin was everything she'd dreamed it would be.

Was it fate?

Dustin drifted back to earth, back to reality.

After making love twice more, Jenna was curled up next to him, sleeping. But he was wide awake, thinking.

Making love with Jenna was special. It was everything he'd dreamed it would be and more. She was a loving, giving partner.

What the hell did I do?

He'd broken his word to Tom.

Guilt rained over him like an Arizona monsoon. He could have gone to his room alone, but he hadn't wanted to. He'd wanted Jenna, and he'd wanted her tonight.

He'd been happy these few weeks at Tom's ranch with Jenna and Andy. For the first time in years, he'd felt like part of a family. It was only play-acting, he told himself, but now he knew that what he'd wanted all along—a loving wife, a good spread and children—would be perfect for him.

But he didn't want to come between Jenna and her brother, her family. And so he had to leave.

He slipped into his clothes, being careful not to wake Jenna. Grabbing his cell phone, he went out to the kitchen so he wouldn't disturb anyone and called a taxi.

"Yeah, I know that Tubac is quite a distance, but I'll make it worth his time," he told the dispatcher. "And I'll double the fee if you're here in ten minutes."

Going back to his room, he threw some clothes into his gear bag along with some of his paints, brushes and pens. He'd ask Tom to pack up the rest of his belongings and get it all to him.

He toyed with the idea of leaving a note for Jenna, but what would he say? I'm sorry?

It would be better if she hated him than for her to have to choose between him and Tom.

Then he waited on the front porch for the taxi to arrive to take him to his lonely apartment over an eclectic art gallery and gift shop.

Jenna reached over to Dustin, but all she found were crumpled sheets.

She didn't hear the telltale squeak of his crutches or sense his presence nearby.

Getting up from the bed, she slipped into her T-shirt and jeans.

She heard the sound of a motor coming from the front of the house, and she looked out the living room window. It was a taxi, and Dustin was getting into the backseat.

She yanked open the front door and stepped onto the cold floor of the porch. "Dustin? Where are you going?"

But he couldn't hear her because the taxi pulled away.

During the seven weeks since he'd left Jenna, Dustin hadn't had his head or his heart in bull riding. The San Antonio Invitational was his first event after recovering from his injury, and he had to ride two bulls and hope that he'd qualify for the short-go round to ride another. If he wanted to be a top contender in Vegas, he needed the points.

He couldn't wait to retire and have his own ranch. But he almost didn't care anymore. If he couldn't have Jenna, what was the sense?

Behind the chutes, he ran into Tom. They hadn't exchanged more than a couple of words since the Wickenburg event. Tom must have sensed him because he looked up from his conversation and nodded toward Dustin, then meandered over to where he was leaning on the chute gate. "What's up, partner?"

"Not much."

"How's the ankle?"

"It's okay."

Tom pushed his hat back with his index finger. "Keep your back straighter. You leaned over his head too much."

"Is that right?" Dustin felt the heat rush to his face. He wanted to punch Tom's grinning face.

"Yeah, that's right. I know you didn't ask for my advice, but that's never stopped me," Tom joked.

Dustin's hands ached from squeezing them into fists. "You stick your nose into a lot of things where it doesn't belong."

"What's that suppose to mean?" Tom asked.

"It means that I love your sister. Now what are you going to do about it?"

"You *what?*"

"You heard me. And I swear, Tom, if you make some smart remark about me chasing buckle bunnies, I'll deck you right here. You know that I'm not like that."

Tom opened his mouth to speak, but Dustin held a hand up.

"I've loved Jenna since I started hanging around with you. And sure, I had some growing up to do, but no woman could ever take her place in my heart. That's why it looked like I was a womanizer. I kept looking for someone to replace her, damn it."

Tom whistled. "I knew you liked her, but—"

"I've always liked her. Now I *love* her," Dustin said strongly, then realized what Tom had just said. "You knew? You knew and you wouldn't let me date her?"

Tom put his hand on Dustin shoulder, but Dustin shrugged it off. "What would you have done in my position, Dustin? My parents had just died. I had to protect Jenna."

"From me?"

"From you! Put yourself in my place. You'd been around, cowboy. Jenna was naive. She couldn't have handled you. Not in high school, not in college. Probably not now."

Dustin wanted to put his fist through something, anything, but nothing was nearby— only Tom's jaw.

"Damn it, Tom. Jenna's going to be thirty years old. When will you think she can *handle* me?"

"Now."

"What?"

"You told me you love her. You won't hurt her now."

Dustin felt a sick feeling in the pit of his stomach. "You're so wrong, Tom. I've already hurt her."

Jenna accepted another flower arrangement from the delivery person and set it on the table to the right side of the door. She'd drop it off at the nearby nursing home on her way to work, just like she'd dropped off all the others.

This was the sixth arrangement in just as many days.

She opened the card and read it. "Please forgive me. Let me explain. Dustin." She tossed it on the pile with the others. Each card said just about the same thing.

It had been two months since they'd made love, since he'd walked out on her. Then suddenly the flowers started arriving. Well, she didn't want to talk, didn't want his excuses. She didn't want to ever see him again.

She'd wasted too many years of her life on Dustin Morgan.

Her face flamed when she thought of how she'd tried to seduce him.

In the end, what had worked? Her old jeans and a T-shirt, a wonderful time at a country fair and some fireworks.

And then they'd had fireworks of their own.

Jenna sighed. She'd thought that Dustin cared for her—cared enough not to leave without saying good-bye or without some kind of explanation.

Had she done or said something that he didn't like?

She was tired of thinking about it, tired of wondering. And now, weeks later, he decided to apologize by showering her with flowers?

"No way," she said, fingering the yellow roses. "No darn way."

Walking into the living room, she turned on the television to watch the Columbus, Ohio, event. It was just her luck that a close-up of Dustin was the first thing she saw. Her breath caught in her chest.

He was being interviewed about his ankle and his rehabilitation. "I'm fine now. I had a nice recovery at Tom Reed's ranch, and the physical therapy worked. I'm as good as new."

The interviewer congratulated him on his

climb back up the rankings to the number two position behind Tom.

"Thanks. Thanks a lot."

His smile lit up the screen, and Jenna could almost believe that he was there with her.

A commercial came on, and Jenna was just about to get some veggie sticks to snack on when she heard Dustin's voice again.

"Oh! It's our commercial," she said, aiming the remote at the TV to make it louder.

There she was in the bikini, walking toward Dustin, and she looked…fabulous.

And then they kissed.

Jenna remembered that it was Dustin who strayed from the script. It was Dustin whose warm, sensuous lips did amazing things to her insides. If she closed her eyes right now, she could relive every detail.

The commercial ended, and she smiled sadly. Even though she didn't go to Europe, she'd had a wonderful summer.

The doorbell rang again. If this was another flower arrangement, she'd scream.

But instead, it was a package delivery service. The delivery person handed her a box wrapped in brown paper. She knew it was from Dustin from the return address. She debated whether or not she should open it or just take it to the nursing home. After debating, she opened it.

It was the painting of the San Xavier del Bac Mission that Dustin had hanging on the wall of his bedroom.

She sat down on the couch, admiring it, thinking and blinking back tears that were stinging her eyes.

The ringing of her phone brought her back to reality. It was Tom.

"I saw that commercial," he said abruptly, without even a hello.

"Wasn't it terrific?" Jenna braced herself for Tom's response. For some reason, she didn't think he'd called to congratulate her.

"What on earth possessed you to do that?"

"The real actress was sick. I was there, so I did it."

"I see," Tom said, then there was silence. Jenna waited to hear what else was on his mind. "You looked good, I have to admit, and it looked as if that kiss was pretty real, and not acting."

Maybe it wasn't acting back then, but she didn't want to talk about it.

"Do you like him, Jenna?"

She took a deep breath. "Why are you asking me that, Tom?"

"Because if you do like him, I think I ruined things for you."

"How?"

"Dustin came to me, talking about a promise that he'd made to me way back in high school."

Her stomach roiled. "What promise was that?" she managed to ask.

"To stay away from you."

"Oh, Tom. How could you?"

"You were only a freshman in high school. Even through Dustin was your age, he was way ahead of you in experience. You were so naive back then. You still are."

"I'm almost thirty years old!" That explained a lot of things, like why Dustin pretty much ignored her. Then again, she was ignoring him. She'd made the same promise to Tom. "I can take care of myself. Don't you get that?"

"But Jenna—"

She cut him off. "But that was a long time ago."

"He'd asked me again about dating you. I told him no again."

Dustin had an attack of guilt, Jenna thought. That's why he'd left her that night. He'd thought he'd broken his promise to her brother.

"Well, you can just tell him that you changed your mind. This is my business, brother dear, not yours."

"I know that now, and I apologize. I had no business interfering. Like you said, you can take care of yourself, and it's about time I realized that."

She sighed. This was such a big mess.

"Do you like him, Jenna?"

"I think I love him."

There was silence on the other end.

"I'm really sorry, Jenna. I'll make things right. I promise," Tom said.

They said their goodbyes and although she knew where her brother was coming from, she was still miffed.

Dustin was constantly on her mind—their kisses, making love with him and the way he left without a word. He could send her all the paintings and all the flower arrangements in the world, and it wouldn't alleviate the hurt that she'd felt when he'd gone off in that taxi.

Tom pulled Dustin to a quiet corner of the cowboy's locker room in the Connecticut arena. "I'm sorry, Dustin…about Jenna. I really blew it with her…and you."

"You're apologizing?"

"I am." Tom nodded. "But you hurt her by leaving without telling her."

"I was thinking of you and your damn edict. Instead, I should have been thinking of Jenna." Dustin held up his hands in surrender. "I love her, Tom, and I think she feels something for me. Now give us your blessing and butt out."

"You have my blessing, but have you talked to Jenna lately?"

"No. She does not want to talk to me. I've tried. I've sent flowers...paintings... I just don't know what else I can do."

"Have you gone to see her in person?"

"No."

"What are you waiting for?"

Tom grinned, then held out his hand, and they shook. With Tom's blessing, Dustin felt like the weight of a Brahma bull had disappeared from his shoulders.

Tom raised an eyebrow. "I know how stubborn my sister can be if she's been wronged. It's going to be an uphill battle for her forgiveness."

Dustin nodded. "But it's a battle that I'm going to win."

It was open house at Wilson Reed Grammar School, and Jenna looked around her classroom and grinned. Parents and grand-parents milled around the room. Every-where were test papers with gold stars. On each child's desk was a folder with his or her work—math, spelling, essays, other tests and artwork. She always thought that art was a wonderful creative outlet for the kids. They seemed to love it, too.

Thinking about art reminded Jenna of Dustin. Actually, everything reminded her of Dustin, and she wondered what he was doing right now.

She was sure he'd moved on. She was just a one-night stand. But wasn't that what she'd been looking for, too? Just a simple seduc-tion?

Now she wanted more. Or perhaps she ex-pected more from Dustin.

Just as the open house was about to end, a man in faded jeans, a chambray shirt and a hat pulled low over his face walked in. He looked at the papers that she'd tacked to the front wall.

She'd know that butt anywhere. Dustin.

Jenna walked the last parent out. She and Dustin were the only ones left. Her heart slammed against her chest, and her mouth suddenly went dry. She cleared her throat.

"Dustin?" she asked.

He turned to her, and every nerve ending in her body started to tingle.

"Is there someplace we could go to talk?" he asked.

She was about to tell him that right here, right now, was fine, but the school would be closing soon. Then she debated as to telling him where he could really go, but she had to give him some points from driving from Tubac to Phoenix to talk to her.

"Are you looking for coffee or beer?" she asked, still not sure if she wanted to talk to him. As far as she was concerned, he'd done the unthinkable by leaving, and there was no excuse.

"Whatever you'd like," he said.

Suddenly she had the urge to go to the honky-tonk on Route 12. She could always watch everyone dance, if Dustin didn't say what she wanted to hear.

"That would be a beer," she said. "Follow my car." She wanted to drive herself in case she wanted to make an escape.

Fifteen minutes later, she pulled into the Cowboy Up Bar and Grill. It was the longest fifteen minutes of her life.

While driving, many things went through

her head, including the fact that Dustin was here in Phoenix, and obviously he was going to try and apologize.

So where had he been for the past two months?

They walked into the Cowboy Up, and a wave of recognition for Dustin rippled through the noisy bar. Fingers pointed, hats were pushed back for a better look, and there were several female squeals of delight.

Good grief.

She looked around, knowing immediately that she'd made a mistake by coming here. Cowboy attire was the dress code, and she stuck out like a sore thumb with her open-house teacher's attire—navy blue suit, a white crepe blouse, a pink paisley scarf, panty hose and sensible shoes.

The hostess was happy to give them a quiet booth in the back, but first he had to sign a menu for her. She held up a felt-tipped pen.

"I'd be happy to," he said good-naturedly, taking the pen. Her hand wrapped around his a little too long, and Jenna raised an eyebrow. The woman didn't care.

He signed his name, gave it back to her and was rewarded with an ear-piercing squeal.

She felt Dustin's hand on the small of her

back as he escorted her to their booth. She steeled herself not to fall for his touch—she wasn't one of his buckle bunnies.

They could just be friends, that's all. Dustin was Tom's friend, and he could be hers, too.

Yes, friends. That'd be her goal.

"Would you like something to eat, Jenna?"

Suddenly she was ravenous. "Wings. Mild." And she was thirsty. "And let's order a pitcher of beer."

He gave their order to the waitress with the midriff-baring top and tight, faded jeans that were torn in just the right places.

"Oh-kay," she drawled. "I'll bring your order just as soon as I can, Dus-tin."

Coming here was a mistake. She could barely hear him above the din of the place. She didn't want everyone knowing their business.

She wanted to leave. Right now. But they had just ordered.

Several people had gathered around their table for his autograph, and he was obliging. He talked to them, laughed with them and had his picture taken with them.

Jenna poured herself a beer, then took a sip. Then she started on the chicken wings without waiting for Dustin. When she finished eating, he was still signing autographs and talking to his fans.

Jenna slid out of the booth, grabbed her purse and left the Cowboy Up.

Chapter Ten

Jenna's phone was ringing when she got home, and she knew it was Dustin. She debated with herself whether or not to have her voice mail pick it up, then finally answered the call.

"Hello?"

"Why did you leave?" Dustin asked.

"Shouldn't I be the one asking you that?" she asked, referring to the night that they'd made love and he'd disappeared into a taxi.

"You're right. I'm sorry. I got caught up signing autographs, but I truly didn't mean to ignore you, Jenna. I didn't. I was almost finished when I saw you walking out the door. Forgive me?"

"Yeah." How could she remain mad at him? He'd gotten her point.

"Can I come over and talk?" he asked.

She'd like to talk to him and would like to see him—longer than she had at the Cowboy Up. "It's late, Dustin, and I have work in the morning," she said instead.

"I won't be long."

Relenting, she gave him directions and paced her living room trying to burn off her nervous energy. About fifteen minutes later, she saw his headlights flash through her front window as he pulled into her driveway.

Now it was time for Dustin to quit stalling and cowboy up. He had some apologizing to do.

Jenna waited until he rang her doorbell. Looking through the peephole, she waited for a few seconds so she wouldn't seem too anxious to see him.

He looked around as he entered the room. "Nice place."

"Thanks. I'm pretty proud of it." She motioned for Dustin to sit on the sofa, and she sat on a wing chair. Smoothing down her skirt, she crossed her legs and waited for him to speak.

"I want to explain about that night…and

why I left." Dustin leaned forward, resting his arms on his legs. He clasped his hands, as if he were one of her students.

She found herself holding her breath.

"I left you that night because I felt guilty about breaking a promise to Tom."

"I know. I talked to Tom and told him that my life is my business and not his." She sighed. "But I don't know why I'm surprised. Tom has taken it upon himself to run my life since our parents died. That's why I moved to Phoenix, but it's still not far enough away from him."

They sat in silence for a few minutes, then Dustin gave a slight smile. "Look, don't be mad at Tom. He just wanted to protect you from me."

"Did he have a reason to?"

Dustin nodded. "I was young and reckless back in high school. And I probably would have hurt you."

She raised an eyebrow.

"Okay. I did hurt you." His sky blue eyes looked down, then met hers.

Jenna shook her head. "I guess I can understand your promise to my brother, but I'm going to be thirty years old in a couple of weeks, for heaven's sake. I'm not Tom's responsibility—I never was. I know he's always found it necessary to protect me, but for you to keep a promise that old…is just plain wrong."

"A promise is a promise. Besides, Tom is damn stubborn. He always was."

"It amazes me that you two have stayed good friends."

"I'm surprised that he suggested that I stay at the Bar R, especially when you were going to be there. The only reason I can think of is that he was doing me a big favor, and he expected me to keep my word."

"Still, you could have said goodbye to me, Dustin."

"I couldn't. You would have pushed for a reason, and I didn't want to come between you and your brother."

"And now?"

"We had it out. He gave me permission to date you."

"That was big of him."

"I—I told him that I loved you."

Jenna was speechless.

"You…love me?"

"Since as far back as I can remember."

Tears pooled in her eyes and threatened to fall. "Oh, Dustin… I love you, too."

His smile lit up his face. "Marry me, Jenna."

"Marry you?" Her voice cracked. She'd been waiting to hear those words for…forever. She didn't know why she didn't scream out "Yes!" but she didn't…she couldn't.

She tried to form the word, but it wouldn't pass her lips. Marriage to anyone wasn't in her plans right now. She'd promised herself adventure and lots of traveling. And there was the possibility of a teaching position in China.

"Dustin, this is all so sudden," she finally said. She had a lot of things to sort out.

"I don't want to waste another second without you."

"I need time to think," she said.

"What's there to think about?"

Jenna suddenly needed to be alone. She needed to figure out if the real Dustin was on a par with her fantasy Dustin. She had to separate fact from fiction.

She stood up. "I need time."

His smiling face melted into seriousness. "How much time?"

She shrugged. "How about the World Finals? I'll give you an answer then."

"That's six weeks away."

"I know."

Jenna snapped her fingers. She had a scathingly brilliant idea. "I think we should date."

"Date?"

She nodded. "I think we should get to know each other more."

"Know each other? I know everything about you."

"You don't know the *real* me."

Dustin sat back, looking serious. "Maybe you're right. Let's date." He stood but seemed reluctant to leave. "I'll give you a call tomorrow and ask you out, how's that?"

She smiled. "I'll accept, so don't be nervous about that."

He held out a hand to her, and she took it. His warmth enveloped her whole being. It felt right being with Dustin, but she wanted to be sure she knew him, not just her idealized vision of him.

But he said he loved me!

And I've always loved him…or was it lust? Or just a crush?

Dustin pulled her toward him, his hands spanning her waist. Her heart beat so wildly in her chest, she thought he could hear it. He kissed her so softly, so tenderly that she thought her heart was going to break.

She didn't want him to leave.

"Stay with me, Dustin. Stay tonight."

"Isn't this awfully soon for a first date?" he asked, eyes twinkling.

She took his hand and led him to her bedroom. Just inside, they dispensed with their clothes in a flurry of snaps, buttons and zippers.

They kissed and held the kiss until they fell onto her bed, tangled in the sheets and comforter.

"I do love you, Jenna."

Tears stung her eyes at the pure honesty of his statement, and she felt content and very much loved.

It seemed to take him forever to deal with the condom, but when he entered her, she felt happy, almost giddy. This strong, artistic, kind cowboy had asked her to marry him.

But was it too late for them? She'd made a life-changing decision to spread her wings, not settle down. But this was Dustin. Dustin!

She gave herself to him completely, yet she held back a little piece of her heart.

The next day, Jenna was called into the principal, Doug Patterson's, office.

"Hi, Doug," she said, slipping into the straight-backed chair in front of his desk. "What's up?"

"I got a call from the superintendent's office. Your application to teach English in China has been accepted. If you're still interested, you'll leave in a month." He shuffled through some papers. "It's a year's position. That's a long time." He looked at her seriously over gold-rimmed half-glasses. "Is this what you still want?"

Jenna's heart started pounding an excited rhythm in her chest. She'd applied for the position months ago.

"This is so exciting, Doug! I'm thrilled to have been chosen." She took a deep breath and thought of all the things she'd have to do to leave. "But I have to leave in a month? It's so soon. And what about my classes?"

"I'll have to get a replacement for you, of course."

A substitute teacher would be with her kids? Jenna's excitement dissipated. Of course they'd need another fourth-grade teacher.

And Dustin! What was she going to tell Dustin?

Her stomach churned. This was her dream job, and she had applied for it before she and Dustin became so close. Before…everything.

She took a couple of deep breaths. What

had happened to the excitement she'd first felt? Now she felt sick.

"Jenna?" Doug asked, standing. "Are you okay?"

"I don't know, Doug. I have to think…"

"Think about it, and let me know by the end of the week." He smiled. "If you change your mind, that's no problem. The super can give the job to someone else."

"If I accept, will you hold my job here?" she asked.

"I'd take you back in a minute, but it might be out of my hands." He nodded. "I'll see what I can do, but I can't promise anything."

Jenna stood. "Fair enough." She held out her hand and they shook. "I'll let you know when I make up my mind."

Jenna's friends took her to the Cowboy Up for her thirtieth birthday. She two-stepped the night away with them and got asked to dance several times by various men.

But none of them were Dustin.

Due to his touring with the PBR, she hadn't seen him much of him since they'd made love, but the phone calls, texts, emails and gifts kept coming. She couldn't wait to watch him on TV, cheering for him until she was hoarse.

Her cheers for Tom were a little more reserved. She was still mad at him for interfering in her life. She'd called him and they talked for over an hour. It would take a while before Jenna would be able to forgive her brother, but it bothered her more that Tom didn't think enough of Dustin to trust him.

When Dustin called to wish her a happy birthday, she'd told him about their gathering. He said he'd be there, but she doubted that he could spare the time to make a pit stop in Phoenix since he had to drive to Laughlin, Nevada, for the next event.

She shook off her problem with her brother and eyed the door like she'd been doing all night, hoping to see Dustin soon. With all the traveling he'd been doing, she'd definitely missed him. Her birthday would be complete if he could join her.

True to his word, he walked in a few hours later. He paused to sign a few autographs, scanned the bar, and spotted her waving to him. His grin lit up his face, then he made his way to where she was sitting with her friends.

After introductions were made, he tweaked his hat at her. "Happy birthday, Jenna."

She smiled, then got up and kissed him.

Her heart fluttered when he whispered in her ear, "I love you."

Her stomach did a little flip. "Isn't that a little soon after our first date?" she joked.

He flashed his trademark smile and chuckled. "I guess you're right."

How could she leave Dustin? She just loved being in his company.

"Dance with me?" he asked.

She took his hand and they walked to the dance floor. It was a Texas two-step, and they fell into line. Dustin was a terrific dancer, and Jenna couldn't stop laughing as she bungled some of the steps.

They danced to a slow song, and her heart melted. Yet she knew she'd have to tell him about her possible job in China soon. Maybe later...

Jenna reminded herself that China would be the adventure that she'd always wanted. It would be an incredible experience.

But as they swayed to the music, she wondered if she could leave Dustin, the man she'd always longed for. Now he'd asked her to marry him. Why wasn't she the happiest woman on earth?

Dustin pulled her even closer to him, as if he never wanted to let her go. His hand tangled in her hair, then he rubbed her neck. She closed her eyes and enjoyed the sensations coursing through her, capturing the memory. She might not see him again for a year.

The song ended and another began. She wanted to dance with him again and postpone what she had to tell him about China. An old Elvis Presley ballad came on the jukebox. The song spoke to her, bringing tears to her eyes.

Jenna moved back and met his gaze. "Let's go find a table. I have something to tell you."

Without waiting for his reply, she began walking toward a free table as Dustin waved off more autograph seekers.

"I'm sorry, everyone," he said. "I'm with a lady, and it's her birthday. I'd be happy to sign later."

They nodded good-naturedly and the crowd dispersed.

"Why did you do that? You enjoy your fans."

"I'll catch them later. Right now, I want to be with you before I have to leave for Laughlin tonight."

She felt elated that he wanted to spend what little time he had with her. She knew how important his fans were to him, and it made her happy that he felt she was more important.

They sat for a while at the table, listening to the rest of "Love Me Tender." Tears threatened to fall as the song spoke to her and her situation. She didn't know how to begin, how to tell him that she'd be gone for a year.

Would he wait for her?

Dustin took her hand. "You got very quiet. What's going on?"

"I have something to tell you. It's important."

His smile faded. "Everything okay?"

"I was asked to teach in China for a year."

Somehow she managed to sound more enthusiastic than she actually felt.

He froze. "When…when did all this come about?"

"Actually, I applied for the job a few months ago, before summer."

"What about your job here? I thought you loved it."

"They said that they'd try to save it for me. If not, I'll just have to find another school somewhere."

Dustin shook his head slowly. "I thought we had something going, Jenna. I asked you to marry me."

"We do, Dustin, but we want different things," she said softly, hoping not to hurt him. "I still have a lot of living to do. I want fun. I want adventure. That's what I promised myself."

"So you're turning me down?" he said slowly, as if he didn't want an answer.

Jenna looked into his turquoise blue eyes. "No. Not exactly." She sighed. "I need more time."

He nodded, but she could tell by the expression on his face that she'd hurt him.

She was hurting, too.

"I see." Dustin looked past her to the dance floor. "When are you leaving?"

"Mid-November."

She could see the disappointment in the slump of his shoulders, the thinning of his lips—those perfect lips—and she wished she could turn back the clock to that perfect day in Wickenburg.

"I'm going to miss the finals. I'm sorry. I won't be there to see you or Tom ride. But I really hope you win."

"I'll win it. I'll win it all. And then I'll retire, find a ranch to buy and…"

She knew what he was about to say. He wanted a stay-at-home wife and a passel of kids. She hoped that he'd get his dream.

At one time, long ago, she'd dreamed the

same dream as Dustin—a ranch full of kids and filled to the brim with love.

Now she was going to China—alone.

She couldn't ask him to wait for her. He should be free to pursue his future with someone who would make him happy.

She was going to China, to teach and travel and explore new places…just what she'd longed to do.

Then why did she feel so empty?

Chapter Eleven

Jenna was going to turn him down.

Dustin tipped his hat to her, gave her a quick kiss, mumbled goodbye and walked away.

As he walked to his truck, his mind was racing. Jenna was going to China? China was a million miles away from everything that he'd hoped for, dreamed of.

This was the worst kind of pain—the kind where his heart splintered into a million different pieces and no doctor could put it back together.

Dustin turned his car and headed north, to pick up Tom at a parking lot by I-10. Then they'd head for Laughlin, driving nonstop.

She wanted to travel, and he was tired of it. All he did was rush from event to event every weekend. He'd been doing that most of his life. After he won the finals in Vegas, he was quitting. He was going to settle down, either with or without Jenna...and it looked like it was going to be without her.

No. He'd wait for her. No matter how long it had to be.

In the glare of his headlights, he saw Tom leaning against his car sipping something out of a foam cup. Knowing his friend, it was coffee, strong and thick.

Tom had barely entered Dustin's truck before Dustin blurted, "What's with your sister going to China?"

"China? That's the first I've heard of that. What's she going to do there?"

"Teach English...for a year."

"Oh." Tom took a sip of his coffee, as Dustin turned his truck toward the interstate. "Where did you see my sister?"

"At a honky-tonk. It's her thirtieth birthday today."

"Oops. I forgot. And I forgot to give her Andy's present—it's a perfect paper in math and one in reading."

"She'll like that."

"Did you get her anything?" Tom asked.

Dustin felt the small box in his jacket pocket that contained a diamond engagement ring. "I bought her something, but then I changed my mind."

Tom dozed while Dustin rolled things around in his mind.

He'd known that she wanted to travel, that she was scheduled to take a trip to Europe and she gave it up to babysit and tutor Andy and take care of him. If she wanted to take *that* trip, he could understand that. He'd even go with her.

But to live in China for a year?

That just wasn't him.

He wanted to turn his truck around and go back and talk to her. He'd bring Tom. Maybe he could talk some sense into her.

Damn. What was he thinking? Tom had interfered enough in their lives.

Dustin had to be the one to talk to Jenna.

Could they work something out?

He was so shocked when she turned him down, he couldn't even think. There must be a solution.

He mulled things around his brain. Then it came to him. They could look for a ranch together—one that was already established—or look at land and build their own. With Jenna actively involved in picking out a ranch with him, she'd be invested in their future together. Then again, maybe she wouldn't want to do this.

"Where are we?" Tom said, half-asleep.

"About seventy-five miles away from Laughlin."

"You want me to drive?" Tom asked.

"I'm fine. Go back to sleep. I'll let you know when I want you to take over."

He doubted that Tom heard him. He was already snoring.

His friend had been on the road for a long time. Even though he'd gotten the money to make some improvements on the ranch, purchase more breeding stock and make the payroll, it had cost him dearly in time away from Andy.

Dustin had gone to Tom's ranch to ride some practice bulls, and he'd noticed how Andy was understandably clinging to his father. It was a tough life for a young boy—a mother who didn't care and was several states away and a father who was always on the road.

That's why he was retiring.

But if the woman of his dreams wanted to travel and he didn't, how could they ever compromise?

* * *

Jenna had fussed with her hair and spent an exorbitant amount of time on her makeup for her next date with Dustin. He was going to drive up from Tubac and she was going to drive down from Phoenix, meeting in the middle at Tom's ranch.

Dustin and Tom were shooting hoops with Andy when she arrived. They all stopped when she parked.

When she got out of the car, she heard Dustin whistle long and low. Butterflies settled in her stomach. He thought she was beautiful, made up or not.

"Aunt Jenna!" Andy yelled.

"How are you, sweetie?" she asked.

"I got an A in math and an A in reading."

"Good for you!"

She nodded at Tom. She'd talk to him sometime when Andy wasn't around. Surprisingly, he stepped toward her, pulling her into a hug.

Tom took Andy inside to make him lunch, and Jenna and Dustin were alone.

She moved in front of him and leaned forward to give him a kiss. He enveloped her in his arms.

"I've missed you."

"I've missed you, too." She felt warm in his embrace.

"So, where are we going? You wouldn't tell me on the phone."

"I thought you could help me check out a ranch that's for sale near the Catalina foothills off River Road."

"You want me to look at a ranch, Dustin?" She furrowed her brow, realizing the significance.

"Yeah." He put a hand on her shoulder. "I'm a cowboy, Jenna. I've been looking at ranches. A pal told me about this one, and I want your opinion. Then we'll go out to eat."

She knew the area they were going to visit. It was beautiful country, and several ranches remained in spite of the condos, apartments and single-family houses springing up around them.

Dustin said that he wanted her opinion, but Jenna knew it was more than that. He wanted her to help him pick out *their* future home.

"Dustin, I don't— I can't—" She took a deep breath and let it out, trying to relax.

"I understand. Your message was loud and clear. But I still want you go to with me."

"But why don't you take Tom with you? He's the rancher, not me."

"I know, but he's not you."

She sighed. "Okay. I'll go."

He smiled. "Thanks."

She closed her eyes, remembering their last conversation about marriage she'd turned him down and said that she needed more time. But the clock was ticking. She needed to let Principal Patterson know if she'd be taking the job in China—or not.

"You're in a good position to win the finals, Dustin. Is that why you're looking at ranches?"

He nodded. "Keep your fingers crossed. Our...er...*my* future depends on that win."

He'd really meant *our* future.

Jenna swallowed the lump in her throat. She hadn't wanted to fall in love with Dustin, but she had.

Hadn't she just want to seduce him? Well, she'd certainly done a great job.

They turned left onto River Road, and Jenna noticed several llamas on one ranch, their heads on long necks observing the vehicles that passed.

They passed by more ranches. Finally, Dustin slowed and made a left turn.

A burgundy-colored ranch house came into view—a sprawling Santa Fe structure with large windows overlooking a corral of horses. Sprawling prickly pear cactus and stately saguaros with their arms reaching to the sky were part of the natural landscaping around the house.

A porch ran the length of the front, and inviting white rocking chairs were positioned at even intervals.

"I love it already," Jenna said. "It's gorgeous and so homey. I can't wait to see inside."

"I hope you like it."

She could just picture herself rocking on the porch next to Dustin and looking at the beautiful scenery. She could get a teaching job in Tucson if she lived here.

Jenna didn't know what to do. She'd wanted Dustin as far back as she could remember. Now, when her dream was about to come true, she was hesitating.

She loved Dustin with her whole heart, but marriage would be the ultimate in settling down.

She owed him a decision.

What on earth was she going to do?

Dustin parked in the driveway next to the ranch house, and a man in jeans and a red Arizona Wildcats sweatshirt waved to them.

Jenna hesitated to get out of the car. She didn't want to like the place.

Aww…she didn't know what she wanted.

Dustin opened the car door for her, and she reluctantly got out.

"You must be Mr. Nichols," Dustin said, holding out his hand. "I'm Dustin Morgan, and this is my…uh…friend… Jenna Reed." He nodded at Jenna. "We're interested in looking at your property."

"Call me Nick. And welcome to our ranch," he said, pumping Dustin's hand and then Jenna's.

"Those horses are beautiful. What else do you run here?" Dustin asked.

"Some three dozen horses—Arabians and quarter horses. Prime stock. And thirty bulls." He looked at Dustin. "I think you know a little about bucking bulls." Nick pushed his hat back. "If you're interested in the stock, we can work out a price."

"I'll take a look," Dustin said.

Nick tweaked his hat brim. "I'm rooting for you to win the finals. It'd sure be nice to have an Arizona cowboy win it."

"Thanks, Nick. I'll try my best," Dustin said.

"Why do you want to sell?" Jenna asked.

"My wife and I want to get out of the business. Maybe do some traveling, visit our kids and grandkids. They're scattered all over the place."

"And this ranch ties you down, doesn't it?" Jenna asked, knowing the answer already.

"Sure does. We're busy day and night."

A stately woman with long salt-and-pepper hair and a warm smile walked out onto the porch. She wore faded jeans and a glittery T-shirt. Her cowboy boots were a bright yellow.

"This is my wife, Amber." He turned to Amber with a big smile. "This is Dustin and his friend, Jenna."

Dustin tweaked his hat and Jenna waved, immediately liking Amber's warm smile.

"I'd recognize Dustin Morgan anywhere. I'm a bull riding fan." Amber walked down the porch steps and shook Dustin's hand. "We put a lot of blood, sweat and tears into this place. Call us sentimental, but we both love this ranch and want to place it into good hands."

Jenna nodded. She didn't blame Amber at all for wanting their hard work to go to people who'd appreciate it.

"Shall we go into the house first?" Amber asked.

"Oh, yes. Absolutely," Jenna said immediately.

They all laughed, but Jenna was drawn to the expression on Dustin's face. He really looked happy and at peace at the same time. This was where he belonged—on a ranch.

Suddenly, she didn't want to look at the house, didn't want to like it.

But she followed Amber on the tour and found that she did like it—very much. From the golden knotty pine to the beehive fireplace, and from the chunky log furniture that came with the house to the rustic chandeliers—it was perfect. The kitchen was a dream. The master bedroom on the first floor was in back and its private deck overlooked a built-in pool and hot tub.

She could picture herself in this house—cooking, grading papers, reading. But would she be happy staying put?

Dustin and Nick went outside to check out the barn and stock, fast friends already.

Jenna felt comfortable with Amber. She was warm and friendly and the type of person who was very open and honest.

It was at times like these that she especially missed her mother. She'd like to talk to her mom about Dustin, about whether or not to marry and settle down, about this property.

Amber motioned to the living room. "I'll bring us some coffee."

"Only if it's already made," Jenna said.

"It is. Coming right up. Make yourself comfortable, Jenna."

Jenna picked a chunky log chair with brown leather cushions and sat down. She had a wide-angle view of the downstairs. Looking around, she decided that she wouldn't change a thing. Well, maybe this, maybe that.

What was she doing? She didn't plan on ever living here.

But she could picture raising a family within these walls with its four bedrooms and four bathrooms. She could imagine their children running through the meadow to the right of the ranch house and riding horses under the watchful eye of their father, Dustin.

She'd keep up the little garden in the back for fresh vegetables and herbs. And the flowers would be perfect for cut arrangements on the circular table over there…or maybe even the mantel. She'd put their Christmas tree to the right of the fireplace. No. To the left, so it can be seen outside, too.

She took a deep breath. She was totally getting ahead of herself, was totally conflicted and wished she'd never came here and seen this fabulous place.

"Here we are," said Amber, returning to the room and handing her a steaming mug of coffee.

"Um… Amber…could I ask you a question?"

Smiling warmly, she crossed her legs and leaned forward. "Ask me anything."

"It's not about the house—it's about… well… I grew up on a ranch, and I know the work involved. I really didn't want to be a rancher. That's why I became a teacher."

Amber nodded. "You're wondering if you'd be happy here."

Tears stung Jenna's eyes, and Amber reached out and patted her hand.

"This was just a cactus patch when we bought it. It was a lot of work—building, making roads, putting up fence, more building, buying stock, breeding. I'm sure you can see that most of the hard work is done, Jenna. Dustin and a couple of hands can do the rest."

"And I can take care of the house," she said, thinking out loud. "Which I'd enjoy. I know I would. And I can still teach. And I can help Dustin in my spare time."

Jenna felt better, but still her mind was racing. Settling on a ranch certainly wasn't in her plan.

But she hadn't counted on falling in love.

When Dustin and Nick returned, they said their goodbyes, and with an invite to return at any time from Nick, they headed west on River Road.

"What do you think, Jenna?" Dustin asked.

"I love it. I love everything about it. I don't think you could find another ranch that had so much care."

"Then you liked the house?"

"I did. I do. It's perfect," she said.

"I have a couple more places to look at. Do you want to go with me?"

"Dustin, I don't think that any other place would top this one."

"I agree, but I think I'll look anyway."

She nodded and spoke softly, "Whether or not we get married, I hope you buy the ranch of your dreams."

Dustin stared straight ahead, but his knuckles gripping the steering wheel were white. Jenna could sense the tension emanating from him.

"You know, Dustin, I've been asleep for thirty years. You might say that I've just woken up."

"You've been busy with your career," he said. "And I know, I know, you want adventure. But did you ever think that marriage could be an adventure?"

She'd never thought of it that way, but it would be a whole new life—and she'd be living it with the man she'd always loved.

"Do you know the name of the ranch?" Dustin finally said, his grip on the steering wheel not lessening.

"No."

"The Rocking JD."

"Dustin, those are our initials!"

"I know."

It was meant to be.

Married life could be an adventure.

The mantras kept rolling around in her head.

"We can't take all the credit." Dustin chuckled. "The ranch was named after the first settler of this area, J. D. Fordham."

She didn't care about the first settler. All she cared about was trying to figure out if she should accept Dustin's proposal or not.

Still, the Rocking JD weighed heavy on her mind. She'd be happy there with Dustin. Wouldn't she?

* * *

Dustin relaxed his grip on the steering wheel and took a couple of deep breaths. He'd thought that seeing the Rocking JD would nudge Jenna to accept his proposal.

Damn it. He'd thought she'd fall into his arms screaming "yes!"

He was pretty sure that it wasn't him. Settling down wasn't in her plans.

"Jenna, I've traveled a lot since I turned sixteen. That's fourteen years. I've given up most every weekend. If I ride in extra events, I'm traveling during the week, too. I want to stay put."

"You know, Dustin…when you go to a PBR event, you're in and out. You don't have time to get a feel for the area. You don't have time to go to museums or the historical society. You don't have time to try the local restaurants or have nice talks with the people."

Her face glowed with excitement, and her eyes sparkled just talking about traveling.

"That's true," he said.

"Wouldn't you like to do all that?" she asked.

"It sounds good." Or maybe it was Jenna's enthusiasm that made it sound good.

Dustin thought for a moment. "If I don't

win the PBR Finals, maybe I'll stick around for another year and keep riding the circuit. You could travel with me. We could explore each city that I'm going to ride in."

"Travel with you for a year?" She tilted her head. "That would be wonderful. Besides, I could keep the buckle bunnies away from you."

He grinned. "If I win the finals, we could still travel, Jenna, to wherever you want. And if you want to go to China, well, could we just visit instead of staying there for a year?"

"Yes." She studied him. "You'd do that for me?"

"I would. But whether I win or lose, I'm buying the Rocking JD. I don't want some-one else to buy it out from under me...us."

"I don't want you to lose it, either. I really love that ranch, Dustin."

"I can't picture anyone else living there but us, Jenna. I don't want to live there alone."

He waited for the big "yes" from her, but it didn't happen. What more could he do?

They drove in silence until they arrived at the steakhouse that Dustin wanted to try.

Getting out of the car, they held hands for a while, admiring the desert landscaping around the restaurant. It was similar to the landscaping around the Rocking JD.

Damn, Dustin thought, stealing another glance at Jenna. He was still waiting for her to be excited about his proposal, but it seemed that she was making her decision a tedious chore. Then again, she was deciding her entire future.

He pulled her into his arms and held her. He kissed her gently, then he broke the kiss and studied her face.

This was his Jenna, and he was all hers.

He hugged her and she rested her head on his shoulder. He heard a contented sigh. Didn't she know how right this felt—the two of them together like this? Together they could weather any storm, tackle any problems, run a ranch...

"You'll always come first with me, Jenna. Not the ranch, so don't worry about that," he said with confidence. "I can think of a dozen guys who could ramrod our ranch when we're not there."

"Our ranch," she whispered, and he could tell she liked the idea. "I could always teach here in Tucson."

His heart soared. Her response was a positive sign.

Jenna wrapped her arms around his neck and kissed him. It rattled him to the core. Couldn't she feel that they were meant for each other? If it weren't for her brother, they would have been together long ago. For sure, they'd even have a house full of kids by now.

"Jenna, I don't want to push you into giving me an answer. It's just that we've both been waiting for each other for...forever. I'm just hoping that you make the right decision, because I don't want to wait much longer."

"You'll have my answer at the finals, Dustin. I promise."

Epilogue

Jenna took her seat at the Thomas and Mack Center on the grounds of the University of Nevada at Las Vegas and settled down to watch the last day of bull riding.

The points were close, and she was already caught up in the excitement that seemed to fill the arena.

Her brother was first in the standings, but Dustin was a close second. The bull rider in third place, Ronnie Bugnacki, could win the event, too.

But they all had to ride their two bulls. One in the long-go, and one in the short-go.

The arena announcer was talking about

how close the race was as the huge screens in the middle of the ceiling showed the top rides of the year by the top three riders.

Today would decide the winner.

Jenna sat on her hands so she wouldn't bite her nails.

Dustin could almost buy the Rocking JD Ranch with the money he'd win. Her brother could pay off the mortgage on his ranch and have enough left over for improvements.

Who would it be?

Jenna fingered the two signs on her lap. One of them was for Tom, the other for Dustin.

Today was the day that she'd promised Dustin that she'd give him her answer. She was content, knowing that she'd made the right decision. It was right for both of them.

As the event began, two "bulls" at each side of the bucking chutes spewed fire from their mouths.

"This is not a rodeo," said the announcer. "This is the PBR!"

The arena dirt suddenly came alive with the letters PBR outlined in fire.

The people in the stands shouted and clapped. It was almost time for the first ride.

Jenna looked at the arena clock behind the

bucking chutes. The digital numbers ticking away reminded her that her life was going to change that fast.

The big screen in the middle of the arena showed Dustin tying his bull rope around Red Wine. Dustin gave a quick grin to the camera, flashing his brilliant smile. The men cheered as many of the women in the arena screamed in excitement. Jenna's heart pounded wildly in her chest.

"C'mon, Dustin. Reach for your dream," she said quietly.

Dustin rode Red Wine for eight seconds and made a good get-off. The arena exploded. His score was ninety. The confetti guns popped as colorful streamers and bits of paper rained over everyone.

She saw Dustin looking around for her. When their eyes met, she waved, and he tipped his hat to her. The heat rushed to Jenna's face as dozens of people looked to see who Dustin Morgan was singling out. Jenna couldn't stop the stupid grin from appearing on her face.

She loved him. She didn't care who knew it. And she'd always love him, no matter what.

She touched the sign that she'd made for Dustin. He had one more bull to ride in the short-go. And the short-go bulls were the toughest yet.

Tom did just as well on Hard Luck and Jenna screamed. She held up a yellow sign with red letters that said, "Go Tom!" He received an eighty-eight.

Dustin had to beat Tom's total score by two points. Then he'd win the finals. He would win the aggregate for the year, too. Two little points.

Jenna sat through eight riders in the short-go. Now it was Tom's turn. He barely stayed on his bull and was hanging off the side of it at the time the buzzer sounded. He wouldn't get very many points due to his style, but he'd get a score. He got an eighty-four.

All Dustin had to do was get a score of eighty-six. It was high, but not impossible on the short-go bulls. He drew a bull named Eliminator, and Jenna hoped that wasn't a sign of things to come.

She held her breath when Dustin nodded his head. Eliminator exploded out of the chute and immediately turned right, into Dustin's hand. A good sign. The bull did four fast rotations, then switched sides and did four more. Dustin stayed on, clinging to the bull like a piece of lint. Finally, the buzzer sounded, and Dustin made a clean get-off, landing on his feet, but then he fell onto the dirt. Eliminator charged, and Jenna screamed, but Dustin was saved by the bullfighters who distracted the bull and got Eliminator to leave the arena.

Quiet settled over the crowd like a thick blanket as Dustin's scores came in. The third judge seemed like he was taking his sweet old time, and Jenna was running out of breath.

Ninety-two! Dustin got his two points and more for good measure. The arena went wild. More confetti spewed out of the guns. Dustin was hoisted up on the shoulders of several other riders. Someone gave him the American flag and he held it high.

Jenna's heart pounded in her chest, and excitement ran through her like an electric shock.

She was happy for Dustin. All his dreams were falling into place.

It was then that she held up her sign. She'd painted it in big black letters on yellow poster board. It said, "I'd love to marry you!"

He saw her and the sign, and a grin split his face. He motioned to his friends to let him down, and he ran toward her.

Climbing into the stands, he gripped her hand. "Are you sure?" he said.

"I'm positive," she said. "I love you, Dustin."

"I love you, Jenna."

He kissed her, and they both smiled.

Jenna put her index finger over his lips. "Let's buy that ranch and fill it with children."

"Agreed!" Dustin exclaimed, then sobered. "I do have a present for you." He pulled out a beat-up envelope from the pocket of his jeans and handed it to her.

With shaky hands she opened it and pulled out its contents. Two tickets to Europe. A cruise! Tears flooded her eyes. "I've always wanted to go on a cruise."

A fan thrust a pen and a program at Dustin for him to sign. Dustin pushed it back. "Hang on. I'm proposing here." He knelt on one knee. "Marry me?"

She held up the sign again. "I'd love to marry you, cowboy."

"Good." Dustin laughed. "It's about time."

Jenna grinned as she pulled him to his feet and into her arms for a big kiss.

Applause erupted around them in the stands, and Jenna realized that the camera was on them. They were on the big screen.

Jenna didn't know what the world had in store, but she knew, just like Dustin said, and as sure as her heart was beating, that their marriage would be an adventure.

* * * * *

HOME on the RANCH

YES! Please send me the **Home on the Ranch Collection** in Larger Print. This collection begins with 3 FREE books and 2 FREE gifts in the first shipment. Along with my 3 free books, I'll also get the next 4 books from the Home on the Ranch Collection, in LARGER PRINT, which I may either return and owe nothing, or keep for the low price of $5.24 U.S./ $5.89 CDN each plus $2.99 for shipping and handling per shipment*. If I decide to continue, about once a month for 8 months I will get 6 or 7 more books, but will only need to pay for 4. That means 2 or 3 books in every shipment will be FREE! If I decide to keep the entire collection, I'll have paid for only 32 books because 19 books are FREE! I understand that accepting the 3 free books and gifts places me under no obligation to buy anything. I can always return a shipment and cancel at any time. My free books and gifts are mine to keep no matter what I decide.

268 HCN 3760 468 HCN 3760

Name	(PLEASE PRINT)	
Address		Apt. #
City	State/Prov.	Zip/Postal Code

Signature (if under 18, a parent or guardian must sign)

Mail to the **Reader Service:**

IN U.S.A.: P.O. Box 1341, Buffalo, New York 14240-8531
IN CANADA: P.O. Box 603, Fort Erie, Ontario L2A 5X3

HRCBPA18R

Get 4 FREE REWARDS!

We'll send you 2 FREE Books plus 2 FREE Mystery Gifts.

Harlequin® Special Edition books feature heroines finding the balance between their work life and personal life on the way to finding true love.

FREE
Value Over
$20

Get 4 FREE REWARDS!

We'll send you 2 FREE Books plus 2 FREE Mystery Gifts.

Harlequin® Romance Larger-Print books feature uplifting escapes that will warm your heart with the ultimate feel-good tales.

FREE
Value Over
$20

YES! Please send me 2 FREE Harlequin® Romance Larger-Print novels and my 2 FREE gifts (gifts are worth about $10 retail). After receiving them, if I don't wish to receive any more books, I can return the shipping statement marked "cancel." If I don't cancel, I will receive 4 brand-new novels every month and be billed just $5.34 per book in the U.S. or $5.74 per book in Canada. That's a savings of at least 15% off the cover price! It's quite a bargain! Shipping and handling is just 50¢ per book in the U.S. and 75¢ per book in Canada*. I understand that accepting the 2 free books and gifts places me under no obligation to buy anything. I can always return a shipment and cancel at any time. The free books and gifts are mine to keep no matter what I decide.

119/319 HDN GMYY

Name (please print)

Address   Apt. #

City   State/Province   Zip/Postal Code

Mail to the **Reader Service:**
IN U.S.A.: P.O. Box 1341, Buffalo, NY 14240-8531
IN CANADA: P.O. Box 603, Fort Erie, Ontario L2A 5X3

Want to try two free books from another series! Call 1-800-873-8635 or visit www.ReaderService.com

---

Get 4 FREE REWARDS!

We'll send you 2 FREE Books plus 2 FREE Mystery Gifts.

Harlequin® Heartwarming™ Larger-Print books feature traditional values of home, family, community and most of all—love.

READERSERVICE.COM

Manage your account online!

- Review your order history
- Manage your payments
- Update your address

*We've designed the
Reader Service website
just for you.*

Enjoy all the features!

- Discover new series available to you, and read excerpts from any series.
- Respond to mailings and special monthly offers.
- Browse the Bonus Bucks catalog and online-only exculsives.
- Share your feedback.

Visit us at:
ReaderService.com

RS16R